THE DAY THEY MADE CONTACT

Luis M. Cruz

THE DAY THEY MADE CONTACT

Luis M. Cruz

Dark Fire Press
New Jersey, USA

Published by Dark Fire Press LLC

Cover illustration: Miguelangel Ruiz (pencils) & Angel Maria Martinez (colors & background)

ISBN (print) 978-1-7335044-6-1
ISBN (digital) 978-1-7335044-7-8

www.darkfirepress.com

First Edition: November 2019

For My Nephew, Noah...

Table of Contents

ACKNOWLEDGMENTS

<u>Acknowledgments</u>

When I was born my parents were told by a doctor that I would not live past my third birthday, that if I did I wouldn't amount to anything but a vegetable, therefore I should be left in the hospital. First and foremost I want to thank GOD for allowing me to live longer than the doctor gave me credit for. Secondly, I want to thank my parents, Luis A. Cruz (R.I.P. every day I wish you were still alive, love you always) and Jenny Cruz for always being there when I needed them, for encouraging me to push beyond my limits and to always excel in anything and everything I do in my life. I want to also thank my brothers, Antonio (Tony) Cruz and Francisco (Frankie) Cruz for their support emotionally and physically. I would also like to give a special thanks to my best friend Mabel Acevedo for her words of encouragement. I don't know why I call you my best friend, when I consider you like the sister I never had. I want to also thank my Editor Yidasia Vargas.

A huge thank you to my family: Grandma Georgina, Grandpa Carlos, Grandma Nicolasa Vega Bonilla (R.I.P.), Aunt Ruth (Cuchie), my favorite Aunt Wanda, Aunt Nelly, Uncle Wilfredo, Uncle Carlos, Uncle Luis E. Bonilla (R.I.P.), Uncle Victor M. Bonilla (R.I.P.), Uncle Edwin (R.I.P.), Uncle Valentine and, Uncle Ray (R.I.P.).

THE DAY THEY MADE CONTACT

I want to give a special thanks to the people who I consider my extended family: Chaka C., Jesus P., Anthony (Tone) G., Edwin (Guido) R., Feliciano (Phil) R., Jackie J., Archie A., Nilsa M., Tomas (Boo-Boo) C., ya'll nine are more than just friends, ya'll family. Christina O., Angel R., Michael G., Luis (A.K.A. Groovie Lou) C., Ashley D, Demaris (My biggest fan), Sabrina, Cynthia H., Luis Q., Stewart W., Marie M., Anna C., Luis Q., Julio A., and Omayra P.

Last but not least I'd like to thank four friends of mine, Miguelangel Ruiz (Artist), Angel M. Martinez (Artist), Henry Simon (Artist) and David Theodore, self publisher of In Da' Hood Publishing and author of "Postal Passions," "Public Access," "Unprotected," and more. Thank you for your encouraging words, I know they came from the heart.

If your name isn't mentioned, please don't feel as if I forgot or don't appreciate you. Its just that I have been blessed with so many family and friends that if I were to put all of your names it would probably be a book of its own.

Thank you all…
Luis M. Cruz

WORD PRONUNCIATION

Draqkorlamaque – Draq-kor-la-maque – Dra/kor/la/mack

Quezok – Que-zok – Quiz/ock

Korlak – Kor-lak – Core/lack

Drakkorlam – Drak-kor-lam – Dra/core/lam

Beklota – Bek-lo-ta – Beck/low/ta

Oubrago – Ou-bra-go –Oh/bra/go

Vayklor – Vay-klor – Vaye/clore

Zeekral – Zee-kral – Zee/crawl

Remoque – Re-moque – Re/mock

Shanstraklar – Shan-stra-klar – Seans/track/lar

T'olask – T-ol-ask

Prolok – Pro-lok – Pro/lock

Brolge – Brolge – Brodge

Pethrasha – Peth-ra-sha – Pet/rash/a

Avoloxzia – Av-o-lox-zia – Ave/owl/lock/cya

Rorlorad – Ror-lor-ad – Roar/lore/ad

Duural – Du-ur-al – Do/ral

Draqkor – Draq/kor – Drak/kor

CHAPTER – 1

It must have been half past seven because John Briggs had just arrived home from work complaining, as usual, about his day. It never failed, every day, six nights a week, he would come home and complain about his job.

"Dad, if you don't like your job then why don't you just quit?" Jason, his fifteen year old son, asked.

"Just because I complain about it, doesn't mean I don't occasionally enjoy it." His father answered.

Jason and his father are very much alike in physical appearance, they both have hazel eyes, they're both slim with medium build shoulders. Both have long black shoulder length hair, with the exception that Jason always kept his hair in a pony-tail, and John, who most of the times had it loose and although he didn't want to admit it, had a receding hairline. However that's where their appearance stops, because Jason had a bronze almost sun tanned complexion due to the mix heritage in his family. His mother, Sandra, who was half Afro-American and Puerto Rican while John was half Italian and American.

John was always interested in talking about politics, but he also had an interest in history, specifically the twentieth century. He felt that the technology that were being utilized then were much more simpler, but yet complicated in many ways and not being used to its full potential. Jason carries with him, in his wallet for good luck, a 1980 American twenty dollar bill which was given to him by his father. There really isn't much of a difference, except that instead of the presidents face being in the middle it was now moved over to the left by a couple of inches. This was done to provide room for the barcodes. It was even printed on smooth, almost wax-like paper. The government claimed that it was made to prevent counterfeiters from producing and distributing their bills out as the real ones.

Now if you were to ask Jason's father, he would say that the bills were made so that the government could keep better track of people. John believed that anything and everything the government did was a conspiracy. That for whatever reason they did things, it wasn't to benefit the people.

On this night Jason and his family were sitting down enjoying dinner and watching as usual, the evening news. Some people would think that while a person was eating he or she would not talk, especially with their mouth full. Well not his father, watching the news during dinner was a big mistake. But on this night Jason, his family, and the entire world will be in shock with what they were about to witness on national television. It all happened so quick, one minute they're eating dinner and discussing politics when all of a sudden the holographic 3D television goes blank for about five seconds.

When the H.3D.T.V. came back on there were no reporters. Even the news itself was no longer broadcasting, it was the same in every station and in every country. The radio stations weren't even broadcasting their usual programs, they were all quiet. On the H.3D.T.V. all anyone was able to see was a large room with high-tech computerized screens and to the sides were walls of panels which had weird almost hieroglyphic markings. As the Briggs family, and every family in the world watched patiently, waiting for an explanation a voice was heard.

"Greetings." The voice said, "My name in your language, is Beklota. We are from the planet Draqkorlamaque, and we come in peace."

At first the Briggs family thought it was some kind of a joke or promotional advertisement for a new television program, until they saw what was talking. This creature was similar to those described in alien abduction books, it had a big oval head with huge black powerful eyes. It had a small slit for a mouth, but it wasn't using it to communicate. Its skin was almost translucent, its body was long and narrow, so were its arms, legs, and fingers.

"My God! Look at that thing, it's hideous." Said Jason's mother, Sandra, as she reached for her husband's hand for comfort. John, who felt her hand touch his, squeezed it gently.

"It ain't hideous and it's not a thing, it's a living being. As a matter of fact, the most remarkable one I have ever seen." Jason said, as he gazed at the H.3D.T.V. in wonder.

The alien, Beklota, continued, "Please do not be frightened by my appearance. Although I cannot see you, my people and I know that you too appear to be different from us." As the alien continued to explain why he couldn't see the people of Earth, which was similar to the way television's and radio's worked, all Jason kept thinking to himself was 'Wow.'

"We will be arriving on your planet in approximately seventeen hours." He then paused for a moment before continuing, "Please do not be frightened by the number of ships, or their size. The mother-ship, Avoloxzia, will remain in space due to its large size. However, several smaller ships will be deployed with permission, to study your Earth's environment. Inside these ships, there will be representatives from my home world who will meet with your leaders, after which they will all report back to me." Yet again he paused. "My people and I are looking forward to meeting with you. Till we arrive, farewell."

The H.3D.T.V. goes blank again for a few seconds, then comes back on with the news reporters who were in as much of a shock as the rest of the world.

"My lord, what the hell was that!?!" Chris Turner said out loud, as he turned to look at his co-anchor Alexandria Booth, who just shrugged her shoulders.

"You're on!" shouted somebody off camera.

"Oh. Yes. We apologize for that interruption, but it was beyond our control." He again looks at his co-anchor as he does every night for her to end the program. But she didn't do anything, she just stared into the cameras with an empty look on her face, so he decides to go on, "Um, we'll have more information for you as it becomes available. For now, this is Chris Turner and Alexandria Booth wishing you a safe and pleasant evening."

As the credits from the evening news were rolling, the telephone rang, "Hello?" Sandra asked as she looked at the phone monitor. It was Jason's aunt, from his mother's side, Natasha. She called to talk to his mother about that thing, as she called it, that was on the H.3D.T.V.

"Oh, hi. How are you doing?" Said Sandra, quickly recognizing her sisters voice, "Yes I saw it… Of course I'm worried… Yeah, we all saw it… Well it looked real, but I guess we'll soon find out…"

As Sandra kept talking on the phone, which sometimes would last hours. John got up from the chair, grabbed the remote to the H.3D.T.V. that was on top of the coffee table alongside the newspaper, which he also grabbed after turning off the H.3D.T.V. He then went and sat on his favorite recliner, which nobody dared to sit on while he was home, and began to read the newspaper. Not one word was heard from him, he just sat their very quietly. It was as if he knew something no one else did.

Later that night, as Jason was getting ready for bed, his father knocked on his bedroom door, "Come in." His father then opened the door and stuck his head through, "Goodnight son."

"Goodnight dad. Dad, why do you think they're coming?" Jason asked, as
he stood by the window looking up at the stars.
John, who Jason can see opening the door wider through the

reflection of the glass, didn't really have an answer. But he gave it a try anyway and said, "I don't know son, but they're coming for a reason. Whatever that reason is, we'll probably regret it."

That night as Jason was trying to fall asleep, his father's words echoed through his head making it very difficult for him to sleep. He was tossing and turning for hours, he would be lucky if he got any sleep at all.

The next morning, Jason woke up earlier than usual. He must have been the first one up among his family, at least he thought he was at the time. But when he went outside to sit on one of the sofa-chairs that was on the front porch, both his mother, father, and even his aunt Natasha were already sitting there, drinking their usual morning coffee.

"What are you guys doing up so early on a Saturday?"

"The same can be asked of you?" His mother answered.

They were either curious or probably couldn't get any sleep he thought, as he went to kiss his aunt on the cheek. Whatever it was he couldn't blame them, after all, Earth was expecting company.

As morning turned into afternoon, all Jason kept thinking about was what the heck his father was doing up so early in the day on his only day off. Of course he knew the reason why, but the aliens weren't going to arrive till at least 3:00 p.m. As the hours continued, everyone in the neighborhood slowly but surely crept there way outside onto their porch, some even went as far as to climb the roofs of either their house or garage. The hour grew closer to their arrival, Jason and his parents were getting anxious and as far as they were able to tell, so was the entire world.

A special report suddenly came on, and its topic was the sighting. The special reports were on every station, in every language. As the reports started coming in about one of the ships, the Briggs family were seeing one first hand. The reporters felt that it was necessary for them to remind the public not to worry and not to be frightened, but nobody was, Jason for one thought that these ships were incredible. Although the ship that was hovering above them wasn't the mother-ship, it was still as large as eleven football stadiums in diameter, if not bigger.

Natasha walked out from under the roof of the porch to get a better view of the flying object, "Would you look at the size of that thing." She said.

"Yeah. Could you imagine the size of the mother-ship, it must be twice as big." Said John, looking up from the side of the porch.

During the special reports, they showed different kinds of ships. Some were colored differently and were of different size and shape, but unique in their own way. Specifically the one that was hovering above the Briggs' state. This ship wasn't like the others, it wasn't oval or saucer-like in shape. It really didn't have any of the traditional shapes people would read about, it basically looked like a silver metallic sphere. The ship made a low humming sound while it was positioning itself, but after it positioned itself the sound was no longer heard.

"Have you noticed anything peculiar about this ship, or for that matter, all of them?" John asked, as he joined his family by the end of the steps of the porch.

"They don't have doors?" She replied as she walked towards her husband.

"At least none that are visible."

"That's dad, always the observer." Jason said sarcastically. Still, Jason could not help but wonder why.

As the days continued, the aliens, or Draqkor as they were called, met with the various representatives of the world. The media kept a close watch on both their appearances, which were slightly different from one another due to their complexions, and also on their progress which was moving at a rather faster pace than anyone in the world had anticipated.

Within one month after their arrival, these beings which looked like passengers from their home world, were given permission by the Earth's representatives and Beklota to come out of their ships. It has been said that if Earth ever made contact with another intelligent life form, that they would perhaps have either a solution or cure to many of the problems and diseases that plague the Earth. But that isn't necessarily true, at least not with these aliens.

The Draqkor were very intelligent, but could not really cure any of the Earth's diseases. They did, however, helped to solve many of Earth's problems, specifically in the field of space travel. In return for their knowledge, they asked the different governments if they can have permission to study Earth's history, especially Top Secret government files.

If Jason's father knew of this exchange he would say that he was right, that they do have a reason for being on Earth. But whether the good people of Earth will regret it or not, still remains a mystery…

CHAPTER – 2

School started about a month ago and instead of everybody talking about what they did over the summer, they're talking about Earth's visitors.

"I thought school was going to be boring this year, didn't you?" Jason asked his best friend, Jesus, as they walked to school together.

Jesus, like his parents, was born in Puerto Rico. But unlike his parents, doesn't speak a word of spanish. Both Jason and Jesus lived just eight city blocks away from the school, so they would accompany each other to and from school. They have been best friends since the second grade, sure they've had their differences throughout the years, but what two friends who call themselves best friends don't?

"Yeah, but I guess we were both wrong." Answered Jesus as they walked by other students who were on their way to school, "Hey, did you hear?"

"Hear what?" Jason asked.

Jesus walked in front of Jason, backwards, with a look of excitement on his face, "You know Mr. Stevens, the history teacher? Well he told my class that a representative from the mother-ship would be visiting our school, he said that it might be Beklota himself. But it isn't certain yet, so don't tell anybody else."

CHAPTER – 2

"That would be so cool." Said Jason, who now had a smile on his face. Both of them now began to walk a little faster, not because of the exciting news, but because they were now going to be late for their first class.

If there was anything that every student in the world noticed that was different about school this year, it was the way classes were being taught. This year not only do the students have to learn about Earth's history, they also have to learn about the Draqkor history as well. Their planet, Draqkorlamaque, is much like Earth, with the exception of its size. It is triple the size of Jupiter and is home to billions upon billions of people, they have even managed to control their weather climate.

The Draqkor have colonized all three of their moons, and have even colonized two of the five planets that make up their solar system, Quezok and Korlak. The fourth and fifth planets, Chabalar and Drakkorlam, isn't suitable for colonization. At least that's what the Draqkorlamaque's history books said, but it doesn't explain why. The history books which the students were studying from, were provided and made by the Draqkor themselves.

Ever since the Draqkor were given permission to leave their ships and walk among humans, they seemed to be observing the people, but then again the humans were also observing them. Most of the Draqkor, through time of course, have managed to make friends with humans. Some have even gone to work or shopping with humans, others have visited homes. The aliens said it was to see, and experience, how humans lived.

Jason, who was dismissed early from school because he was feeling ill, had read somewhere that the Draqkor were studying human behavior by following them around or visiting homes. But never did he think they would visit his home, especially on a day he wasn't feeling well. When Jason arrived home from school he couldn't believe who was their talking to his parents, at first he thought he was imagining things but low and behold their they were, trying his mothers coffee.

"Your teacher called and said you weren't feeling well, what's wrong?" His mother asked as she met him by the door with a worried look on her face.

"My stomach hurts, my head is pounding, it hurts when I swallow and I feel hotter than a cake baking in an oven." He answered, slowly rubbing his stomach counter clockwise.

"You're probably coming down with the flu or something." Said his father.

At that moment his mother placed the palm of her hand on his forehead then his cheeks, trying to feel more or less whether he was faking it or not. As soon as she felt a temperature, and that he wasn't faking, she told him to go to his room and assured him that she would be their shortly to give him medicine.

As Jason laid on his bed waiting for his mother to bring him his medicine, just the thinking of the terrible taste made him shiver, he heard the wooden floor of the house creek. He knew it was his mother because he could hear her mumbling something, but he couldn't figure out who was the other, although he knew it wasn't his father. When his mother came into his bedroom she introduced him to one of the two aliens that was sitting in the living room.

"Jason, this is Oubrago. She says that she can make you feel better quicker than any medicine could." She nervously said.

"Hello Jason, please do not be frighten." The female alien said in a calm and trusting voice, "I am going to place one hand on your forehead and the other on your stomach. Just close your eyes and remain calm."

As Oubrago began to do the things she said she was going to do, Jason caught a quick glimpse of his mother who anyone could tell was nervous. When Oubrago placed her hands on his head and stomach, he looked up at her even though she asked that he keep his eyes closed, but Jason couldn't help himself. He was curious, after all it was the first time he touched an alien or for that matter one touched him. As she felt around to find precisely where it hurt, Jason could feel some kind of heat come out from her hands. It wasn't a scorching heat, it was more of a comfortable warmth. Once she found the spot, the heat got a little warmer.

At that moment, Jason looked at her face again and noticed her eyes were different. They weren't black anymore, they were now glowing an eerie red color. Then after a few seconds his temperature, headache, and everything else was gone.

That night, shortly after Oubrago and the other alien,

who Jason was never introduced to left, he called his best friend Jesus but he wasn't home. Jason felt the need to tell somebody if not he thought, he'll explode. He decides to call his other best friend of nine years, Maggie. Maggie has had a crush on Jason for the last three years, but has never bothered to tell him due to her shyness. He also has had a crush on her for a while but has managed to keep his feelings for her to himself, also due in part to his shyness. Feeling the way she does about him, Maggie believes every word he has ever said. For instance, if he told her that new scientific evidence was recently discovered revealing that the Sun is not the center of our solar system that in fact it was Earth, she would agree without a doubt. It's like the saying goes, love is blind. However, when Jason explained to her what just happened, she didn't believe it. Not until he repeated it three times, word for word, did she believe him.

The next day, at the request of his mother, he remained home from school. Jason has never regret missing a day of school, except on this day. He'd wish he had gone to school because he wanted to be the one to tell his friends about his alien encounter, but he's pretty sure Maggie took care of that the minute he got off the phone with her.

The following day Jason felt like a celebrity, because from the moment he arrived in school, all his friends and teachers kept asking him about was whether or not an alien had cured him of the flu. He was even approached by teachers and students whom he never talked to before, he answered everybody with five simple words, "I'm here today, ain't I?"

CHAPTER – 3

Several months have passed since the last time Jason became sick, and it appears that the school was misinformed about the representative, or for that matter Beklota visiting the school. Instead, the entire school was going to visit him on the mother-ship in space. Jason's school was the first to go to a trip outside of this world, so when the day of the trip came there were photographers and reporters, as well as news helicopters waiting outside of the school. As the different classes started coming out of the school, the reporters stormed both students and teachers with questions about how they felt, such as were they nervous, scared, or anxious. Fortunately, prior to them exiting the school, the teachers and students were instructed to ignore the media till their arrival, this request came directly from the Board of Education Department.

As the classes all lined up, one at a time, two gray colored, large rectangular shaped, ships came down from the partly cloudy sky and began to position themselves above the crowds of teachers, students, and reporters. While they hovered above, all the helicopters that were filming the event lined themselves opposite the rectangular ships, trying to figure out how these objects were going to land so that the people who were going on the trip could get on board. But they weren't the only ones trying to figure it out, because everyone who was waiting on the ground also wanted to know. The two ships were each four to five city blocks long, two stories high, and a hundred and fifty feet wide, therefore preventing them from landing on the ground. When all the classes were lined up, four openings were made from the steel hull of the ships which were hovering seven stories high from the ground. The ships hovered approximately ten feet from each other. on the side of the ships which faced the crowd, the steel liquefied to form steps that reached all the way down to the ground, revealing four dark openings that everyone assumed were doors. From the darkness came four aliens, each standing by one of the doors, waiting for the passengers to board. Jason's class was among the first to enter the first ship, as each person entered they were greeted with a firm hand shake from the aliens.

The aliens asked that everyone walk to the end of the shuttle at arms length, till there were forty-five of them in a row, and say the word 'seat' and one would appear. The seats were formed the same way the steps were, except that the seats rose up from behind each person. As everyone who was suppose to go to the trip were being seated in the ships, there was the feeling of excitement as well as fear. Not one word was spoken, not from teachers or students. Although everybody seemed to be a bit nervous, the aliens made it as comfortable as possible. As soon as everyone was seated, the ships began to lift off and the aliens introduced themselves.

"My name is Vayklor, I am what you would call your

pilot." He said in a calm and confident manner.

"I am Zeekral, your co-pilot." The other said in a similar tone of voice.

"And I am Remoque. I will be your guide throughout this journey." He said in a loud commanding voice, so that all can hear. Remoque, who stood in the front of the ship just behind the seats of both pilot and co-pilot continued, "You are on board one of two shuttles built for this contingency, this one is called the Shanstraklar, named after the first city our ancestors built eons ago. The one that is following behind us is called the Pethrasha, it was named after the first leader of the city. Do any of you have any questions?"

"Yes. Does this shuttle have any windows so that we can observe the mother-ship from the outside, or perhaps the other shuttle?" Mr. Stevens asked.

Mr. Stevens is considered to be one of the schools best science teachers, so he was a little more intrigued than everybody else. Remoque signaled the pilot, who then leaned a little toward the right and stretched his right arm out to touch one of the many buttons on the control panel, causing the entire shuttle to become transparent.

"I guess that answers my question." Mumbled Mr. Stevens.

A few seconds after the Shanstraklar became transparent, so too did the Pethrasha. The shuttles however weren't completely transparent, a vertical steel outline was visible every fifth row of the passenger's seat, it was the same on both shuttles.

THE DAY THEY MADE CONTACT

The Pethrasha, which was behind the Shanstraklar since the beginning of the trip, was now positioning itself alongside. The teachers and students from both shuttles thought that the reason they were now traveling alongside of each other was so that they can see one another, but they were wrong. They noticed that the shuttles were getting closer, they also noticed that the steel outline was changing its form, as if the shuttles were reaching for each other the way the tentacles of an octopus or squid do. When the steel from both shuttles touched, they immediately intertwined and began to pull one another toward each other, till they combined as one large shuttle.

Everybody from one shuttle was now able to interact with the people from the other, and the aliens from the Shanstraklar introduced themselves to the students and teachers of the Pethrasha, and vice-versa.

"I am Tolask, the pilot of the Pethrasha, and this is the co-pilot Prolokba.
You will have to forgive her, she has not learned your language yet." He said as
he pointed at his co-pilot.

"I am for those of you who don't know, Brolge, the guide of the Pethrasha," The third alien said, "Does anyone have any questions?" Many hands were raised, it looked like a presidential press conference where only one person at a time gets chosen to ask a question.

Francisco was lucky. He was chosen to ask the next question, "What happened to the fourth alien who stood by

the door as we were coming in?" He's a rather tall,
heavy set kid, a freshman whom the students have lovingly nick-named flacko, which is Spanish for skinny or slim.

"The alien all of you saw on both shuttles was a hologram." Remoque answered, as Brolge walked behind him and touched a button on the control panel and out of nowhere another alien appeared standing beside Remoque, "And as all of you witnessed earlier, it can and does interact as an individual." Again Brolge touched the button and the alien hologram vanished.

"What is the name of the mother-ship again?" Maggie uttered out loud, without raising her hand.

Both Remoque and Brolge seemed to be taking turns at answering the questions, because Remoque gave Brolge a quick glance, and Brolge answered the question, "As Beklota mentioned on the first day of contact, the name of the mother-ship is Avoloxzia."

Jason, who quickly raised his hand, asked the next question, "How big is
the Avoloxzia?"

That question wasn't answered verbally. Instead both Brolge and Remoque pointed outside toward the front of the shuttle, and there it was, orbiting the planet Pluto.

"I guess my father was wrong." He whispered, thinking that nobody heard him.

"Did you say something to me?" Asked Jake, who was seated next to him. He is
Maggie's younger brother who anyone would think they were

twins seeing as how they looked so much alike.

"Me? No, I was just thinking out loud."

Indeed Jason's father was wrong. The size of the mother-ship wasn't double the size of the ships that hovered above them back on Earth, it wasn't even quadruple the size, it was in fact the size of Earth's North and South American Continents. The mother-ship, Avoloxzia, had all the traditional characteristic features described in the usual alien abduction books. It was flat and round like a frisbee, still everyone was in agreement at how gorgeous it looked when they saw the light from the Sun's rays glimmer from its metallic hull.

As the shuttle started to get closer to the mother-ship, the students, as well as the teachers, were getting excited. But then the look of fear quickly come over their faces as they realized that the shuttle wasn't slowing down, instead it continued its regular speed and course. With every breath the shuttle would get closer and close, and the mother-ship didn't seem to show any sign of an entrance that would let them inside. Just as the shuttle appeared as if though it was going to collide with the mother-ship, Everybody either screamed and covered their eyes or put their heads between their knees, everybody except the aliens.

A few seconds passed and by now everybody expected to hear a crash or kaboom sound before there deaths, but all that was heard was a rather disgusting glooping-slurping sound. When everyone opened there eyes, surprised that they weren't killed, they were already inside the mother-ship.

"Amazing." Jason thought.

The mother-ship changed the molecular structure of its steel hull into a gelatinous liquid, so that the shuttle could enter. After a series of lefts and rights through what seemed to be tunnels made by the mother-ship, they entered some kind of docking bay and everybody was able to see other Draqkor's working on what looked like other ships. These ships, however, were designed differently. They were much smaller than any of their other ships, and they looked like they were designed for only one pilot.

As the shuttle began its docking procedure, the passengers were no longer able to see out because once again the shuttle covered itself with steel, "We have reverted the shuttle back to its metallic form so that you may exit in a safe and cautious manner." Remoque said.

"You wouldn't be tryin' to hide anything, would you?" Whispered Jason.

"Were you talkin' to me?" Asked Maggie, who was standing on line in front of him.

"No." He said, making a mental note of not to think out loud ever again.

Soon as the entire school were gathered outside the shuttle, forty Draqkorlamaque's walked toward them. They stopped five feet away from the crowd of teachers and students, but one continued and asked, "Who is in command of this group?"

At first no one answered, but eventually someone did, "That would be me, I'm
Principal William Gunther." He said as walked through the

crowd with his hand raised in the air, like a student asking his or her teacher if they may be excused from class.

The Draqkor continued, "We will be your… How do you say… Tour guides for the next six to seven hours. If any of you, student or teacher, have any questions about anything please feel free to ask."

As they followed the group of Draqkor's through a long, poorly lit, corridor, Mr. Stevens asked the first question, again, "You communicate telepathically. There's a rumor, back on Earth of course, that you can also read minds. Is that true?"

"Yes we can. But we cannot do it unless we spend at least twenty-four hours with the individual." Replied one of the aliens, although it wasn't certain which one seeing as how none of them bothered to turn around and answer the question directly.

"Why do you have to wait so long?" Mr. Stevens asked yet again.

"It gives our minds enough time to bond with the other individual. If we do it before that time, we would unintentionally shut down the mind."

Jason was relieved to hear that they couldn't read his mind without spending time with him, because some of the things that were going through his head would have probably gotten him in big trouble. He has always been the curious type, so when he asked about the ships he had seen as the shuttle was docking he didn't think twice about it, "For who are those ships that I saw as we were coming in, and why were they smaller than the one's you use to travel from city to city back on Earth?"

After the question was asked, all the Draqkor's that were escorting them around the mother-ship stopped, turned around, and began to walk through the large crowd of students and teachers.

"Well, it was nice knowing you my friend. Don't worry, I'll tell your folks you died heroically." Whispered Jesus sarcastically.

As the Draqkor's approached even closer, their eyes began to glow an eerie dark purple and the teachers and students stood still and got very quiet, it was as if though they were in a hypnotic trance. The aliens, who had now formed a circle around Jason, appeared to be angry, and for the second time throughout this trip—the first was on the shuttle—he was afraid for his life. As the circle of aliens that surrounded him tightened, they began to communicate telepathically to each other. Jason knew they were because he could hear them in his head, although he couldn't understand them for they were communicating in their own language. It was the first time he had ever heard it, or perhaps the only human to ever hear it at all. Their language was unique, he thought, unlike anything he had heard on Earth. The Draqkor language, at least the one that was going through his head, consisted mainly of clicking, hissing, growling and, screeching sounds. As the sounds became louder and more aggressive, Jason dropped to his knees in excruciating pain, it felt as if though his brain was being drilled from the inside out.

THE DAY THEY MADE CONTACT

With his hands on his ears trying to block the sounds, Jason yelled, begging them to stop, but his cries went unheard. Then just when he thought his life was over he heard a loud growling, animalistic sound, a sound that not only frightened him but frightened the Draqkor's that surrounded him as well. The growling came from Oubrago.

There has been a certain bond between Jason and the female alien called Oubrago, ever since the time he came home sick from school. Since then he has never been sick nor has he ever broken or even fractured a single bone in his body, at least not since the time Oubrago healed his knee which he had injured during a football game a couple of months after.

As the Draqkor's backed away, his friends and teachers began to talk and move again. Oubrago, who stood beside Jason, extended her arm to help him stand up from the cold steel floor.

"Are you okay?" She asked in a caring way, "Did they harm you?"

"I'm alright, I'm just a lil' shook up that's all." Jason replied jokingly.

"Shook up?" She repeated in a curious way, as she brushed his hair back with her fingers. It reminded Jason of when he was younger and, his mother use to do the same exact thing whenever he fell or felt ill.

"That is a word which has its own meaning, in this instance however, you are using it to describe how you feel. You are nervous, correct?" Oubrago asked as they walked away from the school crowd and alien escorts.

"Yeah. I'm nervous now, but I was scared a few seconds ago." He said. Jason
then continued by asking her why they reacted the way they did, but Oubrago just ignored him and kept walking.

As they walked through the many different rooms and corridors, in which they had no visible doors but one would form on the steel walls every time one was needed, Jason noticed that in nearly every room there were monitors. One of the rooms he entered seemed to be dedicated to Earth, because every monitor showed every part of Earth right down to the city streets. Another room showed every part of the mother-ship, but the room that interested Jason the most was the one that was monitoring space, it looked as if though they were waiting for something or someone.

Jason asked Oubrago the same question he had asked the escorts, knowing that she would probably hurt him the same way they did, if not more, "Oubrago, those ships that I saw as we were coming in, they're smaller than the ones I've seen your people operate. Who are they for?" Oubrago didn't answer and, thankfully, she didn't hurt him either.

A few minutes of silence went by, but she finally answered him, "The shuttle pilot was suppose to change the shuttle back to its metallic form before entering the mother-ships docking area."

"Then why were they hurting me?" He asked.

"They were not hurting you, not on purpose, instead they were trying to erase your memory of what you had seen. The pilots managed to erase the memory of the teachers and students as they exited the shuttle, but due to the healings I have done to you on several occasions you have acquired certain skills which you are not aware of and probably will not be until you are approximately eighteen years of age. They assumed that your memory was erased along with the rest of them, but unknowingly, you instinctively put up a mental block, preventing them from mentally touching your mind."

Jason, still feeling a little stunned from the pain inflicted upon him by the alien escorts, could only look at her in shock.

CHAPTER – 4

On the day of Jason's trip his parents as well as every other parent who had a child attending Truman High School, and even those who didn't, were glued to their holographic 3-D televisions. Every television station covered the event live, there were camera's in every entrance and exit doorways of the school. Helicopters from every station were flying around, waiting for a ship or something to come down from the sky, and every reporter had one thing in mind, and that was to get the best interview, film footage or photograph of the people who were going on the trip.

All the reporters were practically reporting the same thing but in different words, many television stations were televising film footage from the day they made contact to the day Beklota met with the world leaders. One thing was certain, this is a very special historical event. As the students and teachers began to walk out through the front doors of the school, the reporters quickly began to run up to them while at the same time yelling out questions. But they didn't have time to ask too many, because they were quickly interrupted by a loud thunderous boom and the sightings of two large rectangular shaped objects flying towards the school. As the objects got closer, the helicopters that were flying around all lined themselves up to one side of the school, giving the objects plenty of room to maneuver.

"John, you're gonna miss it." Sandra yelled out to her husband, who was in the kitchen.

"No I'm not, I'll be there in a minute." He yelled back, "Would you like anything from the kitchen?"

"No. Just get your butt over here!" She jokingly demanded. A few seconds later he walked out from the kitchen and into the living room, sat down in his recliner with a small box of vanilla wafers in one hand and a cup of milk in the other.

"And to think Sandra, you almost didn't let him go." He said with a mouth full of cookies.

"Well you're damn right I almost didn't" She said while leaning forward and snatching a cookie from his hand, then sat back down, "If it weren't for Oubrago, who assured me that she would keep an eye on him, I don't think I would've."

"What's there to look out for?," He said as he paused to take a sip of milk,
"Jason's fifteen years old, he can look out for himself."

"You're probably right, he can... On Earth, not in space." She said in a harsh derision.

After a minute or so of looking at the news and trying to find their son in the crowd of thousands of other students and teachers, they finally see him, "There he goes, there's Jason." Sandra said frantically, as she pointed at the H.3-D.T.V.

Although they both only caught a quick glimpse, that

was enough to satisfy them, even though the glimpse they saw was of him boarding one of the shuttles. Once everyone was on board, the shuttles took off.

John and Sandra both were quiet for awhile and both were worried about the kids, but they weren't the only ones, so were the billions of people in the world. These weren't just kids, these were the children, although just a handful, of mother Earth.

After Oubrago told Jason that he had acquired certain skills, which he would have to learn how to use, they met up with the rest of the school who- didn't even notice they were gone. One of the things that everybody found most interesting, was the way doors would appear out of pure solid steel. The steel would liquefy, much like the shuttles did, to reveal either rooms or corridors that lead to rooms.

"Oubrago, I have a headache." Jason said as he placed his left hand on his
forehead, as if trying to prevent it from falling.

"Jason, I would like for you to try something," Said Oubrago, as she pulled his left hand from his head, "I want you to close your eyes, and concentrate. Imagine, if you will, that the headache has a solid form or shape. Now place both of your hands on the side of head and pretend that you are pulling the headache, which now has a form, away from your head and is now on the palm of your hands." While Jason did what Oubrago instructed him to do, no one noticed, it was if though he and Oubrago didn't exist.

"Can you see it?" She asked.

"Not only can I see it, but I can feel it throbbing in my hands."

"Good," She said, "Now crush it."

Jason, who looked like he was palming a basketball, clenched his hands together. While in his mind, he was seeing his hands crushing a bubble containing red electrical sparks.

"Wow. That was awesome," He said, "My headache is gone. Thank you Oubrago."

She then put an arm around his shoulders and continued to walk towards the group, who were just a few yards down the corridor, and said, "You do not have to thank me. You were the one who did it, not I."

"But how?"

"That is but one of the things you will have to learn." She answered, "Now go,
you will be leaving very shortly."

"But I haven't even seen what my school mates saw, I've spent the entire day walking around the ship with you." He said.

"I apologize for keeping you away from your friends, but you did see what they saw and, as far as they are concerned, you were there with them all day." She said.

"How's that possible?"

"You see while we were, as you said, walking around, I implanted in all their minds that you were there. Some even had conversations with you."

"Yeah, but I wasn't there. So if they ask me anything

about this trip, I won't know."

"But you will know." Said Oubrago, as she placed her hands on his forehead, causing his mind to be flooded with images of the most important things his school mates saw and talked about.

"I thought your people couldn't read our minds without spending time with the person?"

"My people can do more than you think." She said as she turned to walk away from him, "Keep in mind, that not all of us are what we say. We may look and do the same, but we are not."

"What do you mean?" Asked a now puzzled Jason.

Oubrago then stopped, turned to look at Jason, and lifted one hand to point at the students and teachers who were now boarding the shuttles, which were again separated to return back to Earth. "That conversation will be discussed another day. I will see you soon. Send my regards to your parents, and tell them I will visit in one week from today."

Although Jason was among the last to get in the shuttle, he still managed to get a seat next to his best friends, Jesus and Maggie. All they kept talking about was the trip, and that was the topic of the month because when they exited the shuttle, which were hovering a couple of stories higher than before in front of the school, the reporters were still their. Some of the teachers and students decided to talk to the reporters, others went straight home to tell their families and friends, Jason was one of them.

Jason told his parents everything that happened during the trip, he was surprised that he could remember certain things so clearly and with such detail. Things he didn't see with his own eyes, but through the eyes of others. Like the meeting between the school and Beklota, how he shook hands with every teacher and student, Jason even felt the hands of Beklota on his.

Even though Jason told everything to his parents, he didn't tell them about the pain the Draqkor's inflicted on him. He also didn't tell them about the things Oubrago did and told him because he had a feeling that if he did, they would probably freak-out.

CHAPTER – 5

Winter 2047.

Above Washington D.C. is a dark blue triangular shaped ship which has been gathering top secret government information from all over the world, and relaying the information to the mother-ship, Avoloxzia. The triangular ship is one of the smallest ships deployed to Earth and the latest one, which arrived six months ago. Its name cannot be translated in English or any other language, so the people of Earth have named it the "D.C." ship, which stands for the "Data Collector."

The D.C. ship has only two decks, deck one is for working stations, the bridge, and the engineering, while deck two serves as the living quarters to all one hundred twenty-five of the crew. Seventy percent of its crew are mainly scientists, while the other thirty percent are comprised of soldiers and engineers. The crew work in two, twelve hour shifts.

"These humans have had a very interesting evolutionary process, from a historical point of view." Duural said to the Captain of the D.C. ship and, lead scientist, Zard.

Duural is second in command of the D.C. ship, and assistant to Zard. He is also responsible for all the data that is gathered from every scientist on board the ship, which he therefore reports to Zard.

Each and every scientist is responsible for gathering data on a specific time period of Earth, from the much theorized primordial ooze, to the day before they arrived. After the data is gathered, the scientists then transfer the information to one of the one hundred computer terminal workstations which are located throughout the ship every forty to fifty feet.

The transfer process of the information isn't done physically, instead it is done mentally through a mind-link between alien and computer. The aliens, upon gathering the information, whether it be by touch, smell, taste, hearing, or seeing, go to a computer terminal which extracts the information. The computer terminal has no monitor, but does however have a holographic three dimensional keyboard with alien markings. The monitor is replaced by visors that the aliens use to either retrieve, or input information. The visors have two steel-like needles, one for each eye, that retrieves the information directly from the alien by piercing through the eyes. Every detail of every second is then transferred to the computer, until either the assistant scientist or the lead scientist can review the data. The mind-link process is painless to the aliens.

After a scientist has completed gathering information on a specific time period, he or she, move on to the next available time period. Duural's responsibility is not to evaluate human evolution, but to study whether or not the human race were unknowingly, technologically, influenced by an alien race and/or have ever been contacted or visited by an unknown alien race.

"Explain." Said Zard, while plugging himself to the visor.

"They have fought with each other throughout their existence, have been slaves due to the color of their skin or beliefs, have nearly destroyed their planet on more then one occasion. But what I find most interesting is their ability to work together in times of need and the things they can accomplish when not in war, also their thirst for the unknown and unexplainable."

"Show me what you have gathered thus far." Said Zard.

Duural pressed a few buttons on the holographic keyboard, causing the computer terminal in which Zard's mind was linked with to be flooded with images and documents of Earth's past. It takes only a couple of seconds for the data to be transferred from computer to alien, and vice-versa.

"Beklota needs to view this data immediately, and it must be presented to him in person." Zard said as he took off the visor.

"Shall I order a shuttle to be prepared to take you to the Avoloxzia?" Asked Duural.

"Yes."

The Avoloxzia is in a low standard orbit behind the planet Pluto, no human has visited the mother-ship in over three months therefore, no one is aware of the shuttles that are constantly traveling to and from the planet. On the bridge of the Avoloxzia stands Beklota, surrounded by the bridge crew, lost in thought as he watches the shuttles of different size and shape.

"Beklota, Sir." The second in command of the Avoloxzia said, "Scientist Zard is here to see you."

"Thank you Commander Kralo." He said, still staring out at the planet.

Beklota, after a few seconds, walks away from the window to greet Zard, who has been standing their since his introduction by Commander Kralo. The window, when not in use, immediately covers itself with steel.

"Zard, what brings you here?"

"I came to bring you an update on our search." Said Zard.

"Then, you have found them?" Asked Beklota as they both walked out from the bridge.

"No." He answered reluctantly.

"Then what kind of information did you bring me?"

"I bring you information about the people of Earth. How they were in the past and, how they reacted toward one another."

"Really." Beklota said as he led Zard to a computer terminal, "Come, show me."

Beklota and Zard were now mind-linked to the computer terminal, and Beklota was now getting the same information that Zard had received from Duural.

"This data will perhaps one day be of some importance," Said Zard, "But why did you not send it through our secured computer net?"

"I needed an excuse to get away from the cold temperature of Earth."

"Ah, yes. I have forgotten about the Earth's ever changing climate."

"I could not help but notice that, on the bridge, you were staring out at the planet Pluto. I take it your plans for colonizing the planet is going well." Zard said as Beklota disconnected himself from the computer terminal.

"Not as well as you may think." Responded Beklota, sounding a bit disappointed.

"Come," He said, "I will explain it to you on the way back to your shuttle."

Together they walked, Beklota being saluted by everyone who walked by him, talking about the advantages and disadvantages of colonizing the planet, "Seventy-five percent of the planets surface is rock mixed with ice. Pluto's atmosphere also contains nitrogen and methane with traces of carbon monoxide, making it very difficult to do anything with the planet, seeing as how its temperature is colder than seventy kelvin." Beklota explained.

"Why not simply use the Environmental Climate Controller on the planet?" Asked Zard.

"If I were to use that, the people of Earth would notice. Thankfully they are unaware of what is going on, due to our orbit behind the planet. Therefore, making it impossible for their improved Hubble Telescope to pay us any attention."

"Are they not concerned about your whereabouts?"

"Not at all, since I mentioned to them that the Avoloxzia would be going back to our home planet every so often for minor upgrades and crew rotations."

"When did you tell them you would return?"

"I informed their representatives that the Avoloxzia would be returning during there spring season."

Thirty minutes has passed and both Beklota and Zard are finally at the shuttle-bay, waiting for the pilots to lower the shuttles passenger ramp which they did after a couple of seconds.

"I will keep you informed on our progress through the computer net.
Farewell, Beklota." Said Zard as he stood by the shuttle door saluting him.

"Farewell Zard." Beklota said as the shuttles steel ramp sealed the doorway and took off.

Once more Beklota is on the bridge looking out at the planet through the same window as before, thinking to himself yet again. This time with a much more clear thought on the humans, as he again watched the shuttles travel back and forth.

CHAPTER – 6

It's Christmas morning and in the Briggs house preparations are being made to celebrate not only the holiday, but also Jason's birthday. Sandra is busy in the kitchen baking her traditional fudge cake and a couple of apple pies, not to mention the lunch and snacks, while Natasha prepared the living room with birthday balloons and party stringers. Although there was a lot of protest from John, about the removal of his recliner from the living room, he lost, like he does every year. The recliner along with the entire living room furniture were taken to the attic, to provide space for the kids to dance.

After John and Jason took the things to the attic, they both sat down and rested on one of the couches. "Jason, what are your plans?"

"Well dad, if you must know, I plan to party all night long." Replied Jason with a smirk on his face.

"No Jason. I mean what are your plans for the future? For example, after you graduate are you going to college?"

"I don't know. I never bothered to think that far ahead."

"Well perhaps you should, after all, your mother and I won't be around all your life."

"Maybe not all my life, but I would hope you'll be

there for all the important things." Said Jason with a serious look on his face.

It was now quiet in the attic and John took that as a good sign that he got into his son's head, made him think about the future instead day to day. John also thought about the future in this moment of serenity, he thought about whether or not the aliens were sincere in what they said about assisting humanity advance technologically. He also thought about growing old with his wife and watching Jason grow up and have a family of his own, and becoming whatever it is he was hopefully now thinking.

"John, Jason, would you please come down here and help me decorate the living room." Yelled Natasha from the foot of the stairs.

"I guess we should go help your aunt." Said John as they both got up from the couches.

"Yeah… So much for resting for awhile, hey dad."

As they walked down the stairs, slower than turtles, the telephone rang and, of course, Sandra answered it. She talked with the person on the other end for a long time before hanging up. "Jason, that was Maggie calling from her house. She asked if you can go pick her up in about a half hour." She said with a sort of wicked smile on her face.

"Saved by the bell dad, or rather the ringing." He said, grabbing his black leather trench coat and speed walked out the front door.

"What's with the smile honey?" John asked while hanging a birthday balloon.

"You never mind the smile, just keep hanging the decorations." She said as she disappeared behind the kitchen door to continue her baking.

It took Jason twenty minutes to get from his house to Maggie's, and all the while he thought about what he and his father discussed in the attic. He thought about it so much, that he nearly walked passed Maggie's house. Her house was similar to his, except that it was a two family house. Maggie's grandmother lived on the first floor, while she and her family lived in the second floor.

Jason opened the gate and walked up the two steps leading to the porch, where he then pressed the second floor doorbell. He waited a few seconds before pressing it again, just as he was about to press it a third time, Maggie finally opens the door. She answered the door wearing only her gray sweat pants with a matching gray turtleneck sweater, and her beat up white and gray sneakers. Taken by surprise with her appearance, he hadn't even noticed that her sneakers had no shoelaces. Her dark red hair, which she normally would have loose, was now wrapped around her head.

"You're not ready yet?" Asked Jason, sounding a bit childish.

"And a Merry Christmas/Happy birthday to you too." Maggie said sarcastically.

"Oh, I'm sorry. Its just that well, never mind." He said, feeling like an idiot, "Merry Christmas."

"Ready when you are." Maggie said in a very cold

tone, as she grabbed her coat and book bag that were hanging behind the door.

"Don't you wanna change first?"

"What's wrong with the way I look?" She asked as she looked down at herself, "Anyway I got a change of clothes in the bag."

Jason knew the minute they walked out the gate that it would be the longest twenty minutes of his life going back home, unless he could figure a way to break the tension between them. He thought of everything and anything, but he knew that no matter what he tried, probably wouldn't work. But he tried anyway.

"What are your plans?" He asked her.

A few seconds of silence went by before she answered, "What do you mean by that?"

Relieved that she no longer seemed to be upset at him, at least not too much. He makes a mental note to thank his father for asking him the same question, which he now used to break the tension, and decides to continue with the conversation. "I mean what are your plans for the future?"

"Well?" He persistently asked after yet a few more seconds of silence.

"Don't rush me, I'm thinking." She said, "I know, I want to get married with 'Mr. Right' have two or three kids and maybe a dog and/or cat, and live in a big house. I would also like to have a successful career or maybe even my own business."

"What about college?"

CHAPTER – 6

"What about it?"

"Aren't you going to college?"

"No. College is not for everybody." She said, "you said that yourself once, remember?"

"Yeah, I remember. But it's different when your parents expect that of you."

"They want you to go to college, don't they?"

"My parents haven't said anything yet, but I'm sure they're thinking it."

He said disappointingly, "They probably expect me to attend New York

University, like my father did."

"Jason, if you didn't attend college, what would you do instead?"

"I'm not really sure. But I've been thinking about the military, especially about being a pilot."

"But Jason, nobody is fighting against each other, there isn't a war in the world and there hasn't been one in years. The military is practically useless, why would you want to waste your life on a useless career for?"

"That's exactly why, because it is my life. That, and the new flight crafts they have."

"What about the new flight crafts? What's so special about them?" She asked as they waited for the street light to change.

"Have you seen these crafts?"

"Nope."

The street light took a long time to change, there was

no cars coming or going, so they both make a run for it.

"Well let me tell you what I've read about them. These aircrafts, which were designed after the F-18 fighter jets of the late twentieth century, they were made by the military from Draqkor technology. They will have the capability to fly on Earth as well as space, they can fly as far as Mars in a matter of minutes compared to the months that it takes now, at least that's what I read in the article. The Draqkor's are currently developing a fighter jet similar to their own fighter, these will be different because they will be able to change shape according to the imagination of the pilot." He said excitingly.

Maggie could see that his mind was made up, that no matter what she or his parents say, Jason was still going to join the military, "And where did you read this at?" She asked.

"I don't remember, it was in an article I read in the newspaper a few days ago."

They were both now on the front porch and Jason, after searching his pockets, remembers that he left his key's inside and must now ring the bell. "Wait Jason, don't ring the doorbell yet." She suddenly said, preventing his hand from touching the doorbell by pulling his arm down.

"Why not?"

"Because…" She said as she tried to think of an excuse, "Because I want to give you your birthday present now." Yeah, that's it, she thought to herself.

Maggie has always been shy when it came to letting Jason know how she felt about him, but today she needed to prove herself. They're both almost the same height so she stands in front of him, face to face, and says, "Close your eyes and don't open them till I tell you."

Jason closes his eyes and feels her hands touching his face, softly caressing him. He feels Maggie pulling his face closer to hers, feeling her breath on his face. Figuring out what his gift was going to be wasn't so difficult anymore, at least he thought it wasn't. He began to feel something else, some kind of mental impression, but couldn't figure out what it was even though it felt very familiar. Maggie, at this moment, felt so proud of herself. Here she was, standing in front of Jason, ready to kiss him without getting nervous, backing away or giggling.

"Oubrago." Whispered Jason.

"What!?!" Said Maggie while pulling away from him.

"Oubrago… She's coming." He said, looking around at everyone in the street.

"You are mistaken Jason, I am already here." Oubrago said.

"Where?"

"Jason, who are you talking to?" Asked Maggie.

"I'm talking to Oubrago." He said, "Can't you hear her?"

"No." Maggie couldn't hear or see Oubrago, even though Jason could, at least, hear her. Unknown to Maggie, Oubrago was communicating with him telepathically.

"Jason, she cannot hear me. Therefore, I would suggest you speak only with your mind."

"How?"

"How what Jason?" Maggie asked, annoyed at the fact that she couldn't hear whatever it was that Jason was hearing, and that her chance to let him know how she felt about him was now ruined.

"Simple Jason." Said Oubrago, "Just think about what you are going to say, but do not say it verbally."

"Like this?" He asked mentally.

"Yes, very good."

"Where are you?"

"That is for me to know, and for you to find out."

"Are you close?" He asked while walking pass Maggie, down the porch steps, looking all over the street again.

"Closer than you think."

"Helloooo!?! Earth to Jason." Said Maggie, taunting him, "There's nobody out there... Okay, you know what, I'm going inside."

Maggie, after knocking on the door, went inside wanting to slam the door but didn't, for she knew it would be rude and this wasn't her house. Jason didn't even notice that she had gone inside, he just stood out there communicating telepathically with Oubrago.

"Can you give me a hint?"

"No. But if you concentrate hard enough, you will find me."

Jason closed his eyes, to focus better and not be distracted with the people and vehicles that were passing by the house. Suddenly, Jason opened his eyes and hurried up the porch steps. "I know where you're at!"

CHAPTER – 6

"Really?" Oubrago said in disbelief, "Then where am I?"

"You're in the kitchen with my mother, in fact you're helping her with the baking."

"How do you know that?" She curiously asked.

"Because I'm watching you." Said Jason out loud, leaning by the kitchen door with his arms crossed.

Both Sandra and Oubrago were startled, especially Oubrago who should have sensed him coming towards the kitchen.

"I didn't know you were standing their watching me honey." Sandra said.

"Mom, I didn't mean--"

"Do not try to explain Jason, you will only confuse, perhaps, even frighten her." Oubrago mentally interrupted.

"You didn't mean what, Jason." Sandra wanted to know.

"Never mind mom, it was nothing." Said Jason.

"I told you Mrs. Briggs," Maggie said, coming into the kitchen, "He was acting kind of nutty outside as well."

"Sandra I will take Jason for a walk, as agreed during our earlier conversation." Oubrago whispered, so that Jason wouldn't hear.

CHAPTER – 7

Oubrago and Jason walked out the front door and stood by the porch steps for awhile, not knowing where to go. As they stood out there, it began to snow and Jason walked down the steps to feel the snowflakes land on his face, he then looked up at the sky, opened his mouth, and stuck his tongue out. Oubrago, after watching Jason for a few minutes, walked beside him and stared with curiosity.

"Jason, what is the purpose for you standing there with your tongue sticking out of your mouth?" Asked Oubrago, as she circled around him.

"There is no purpose Oubrago." He said, "But it's fun to do, maybe you should try it."

Oubrago, imitating Jason, also looked up and stuck her tongue out to catch the snowflakes, "The snow tastes like water, why is that?"

"Because that's what it is, it's water in a solid form."

Jason began to walk, without knowing where to go. He was so excited about the fact that it was snowing on Christmas, his birthday, not to mention that the last time there was a white Christmas was in the year 2013.

"Where are we going Jason?"

"This is the way to the local mall. I thought you might

be interested in seeing the different decorations the department stores put on display to celebrate this joyous of all holidays and, not to mention, attract more paying customers than usual."

As they both walked, the snow accumulated and Oubrago couldn't help but observe the way people reacted, some hate it, others loved it, particularly the children. She noticed the way the children played with it and created different things with it such as snowmen, igloo's, and snowballs, while the adults cursed at it and brushed it off from their vehicles and property walkways. As they passed Maggie's house Jason is suddenly hit with a snowball on the back of his shoulders. Oubrago turned around very quickly at the direction from which the snowball was thrown, her hands were clenched into a fist which were glowing a bright blue color.

"No Oubrago, don't." Said Jason, as he stood in front of her, "He didn't hurt me."

"He did not hurt you?"

"No."

"But at the velocity of the impact, you should at least be suffering from an injury."

"But I'm not." He said, grabbing a handful of snow and molding it into a ball. He then tossed the newly formed snowball at her arm, to demonstrate that it didn't hurt, "Besides, I know him. He's my friend, Jake."

"Jake?" A now calmed Oubrago asked.

"Yeah… Jake. Maggie's younger brother."

Jake sprinted toward Jason and Oubrago to apologize

for the snowball and to wish Jason a happy birthday, and a Merry Christmas. At least that's what Jason thought, but apparently he was wrong.

"Hey Jason, how's it goin'." Jake said, patting Jason on the shoulder.

"I'm alright. But why did you hit me with a snowball?"

"I don't know… Consider it an early birthday gift or something." He said, with a smile on his face.

"Ha-ha, very funny." Jason said realizing that he was being rude, "Jake, this is Oubrago and vice – versa."

"I've heard a lot about you Oubrago." He said while extending his hand to shake hers.

"I, unfortunately, have not heard enough about you." She replied, nearly

forgetting that humans normally greet each other by shaking hands.

"Jake am I gonna see you tonight at the party or what?"

"Hell yeah." He responded very excitedly, "Although I might be a little late, so please let my sister know that."

"Alright I will, see you later on tonight." Said Jason while slowly walking away.

"It was nice meeting you Oubrago." Jake said as he hurried back towards his friends to continue the snowball fight.

"Likewise Jake." She said as she followed Jason.

It was quiet for a little while, Oubrago in the meantime

kept observing the people play with the snow. She grabbed some snow from the hood of a car and began to mold it, the same way Jason did. Jason wasn't paying any mind, therefore unaware what she was planning to do with now some-what spherical snowball, she tosses it at his back.

"Hey! What was that for!?!" He said arching his back as some of the snow managed to get in his coat.

"It seemed appropriate, seeing as how you threw one at me."

"Yeah." Surprised that she threw him with a snowball, "But that was to demonstrate to you that it doesn't hurt to get hit by one."

"The one that I hit you with, did it hurt?" Asked Oubrago, concerned that she might have injured him with the snowball.

"No, of course not." He said, as she rubbed his back, specifically the area she hit him in, "Its just that I didn't expect you to hit me back."

"I am very sorry, but it's just that I wanted to do what they are doing." Pointing at a group of people, adults and children, throwing snowballs at each other.

"So, you wanna play, huh?" He said, grabbing snow from the ground and making a snowball which he then flung at her.

Oubrago and Jason played with the snow for hours, both loosing track of the time. During that time, he taught her how to make a snowman and an igloo. After realizing that it was getting late, they both decided to start heading back to the house.

"Oubrago, I'm sorry we didn't have time to go to the mall. I'm sure you would've enjoyed it."

"Do not concern yourself Jason, there is always another day."

As they walked home, Jason is telling Oubrago about everything she would have seen in the mall. He begins to describes every Christmas decoration, when suddenly Oubrago interrupts him.

"I apologize, Jason, for cutting you off and for changing the subject. However, I feel that I must tell you the truth about myself."

"What do you mean?"

"Come with me and I will show you."

She led Jason through an old alley, the snow was untouched and much thicker, making it difficult but manageable to walk. Oubrago stopped about halfway in and stood there, very quiet. She kept looking up at the rooftop and at both of the entrances of the alley in an almost paranoid way, she then grabbed him by the hand and hid between two dumpsters.

"Well, are you going to show me or not?" An impatient Jason asked.

"Yes. But first I must tell you that what I am about to do to you will not harm you."

"What are you going to do to me?" He asked, nervously taking a step back.

"Just watch." Oubrago placed two of her fingers on each side of Jason's head, his temples to be exact. Jason felt a slight tingle on his temples, which was being caused by Oubrago's fingers. He no longer saw snow nor felt cold, in fact wasn't even on Earth, at least not mentally.

In his mind, he was standing near the edge of a mountain peak, looking down at a very dark blue river several hundred feet below him. At first, he thought he was seeing something Oubrago had seen somewhere on Earth, that is until he looked up at the bright blue sky and saw two Sun's.

"Where am I?" He asked, quickly moving away from the edge.

"You are on my planet, Drakkorlam." Oubrago Answered.

"How is that possible?"

"I have established a mind-link between you and I which allows you to see, hear, touch, smell, and taste everything I have. Or at least the things that I can remember."

"Wait a minute, slow down." He said, as he leaned down and sat on rock about four feet away from the mountain's edge, "I don't understand, I learned in school that your people came from the planet Draqkorlamaque. Now you're telling me that you came from this planet."

"That is correct."

"Now I'm really confused."

"Do not be, Jason." Oubrago, trying to assure him, said. "Do you not remember what I said to you on the Avoloxzia, on the day of your school trip, just before you boarded the shuttle?"

"Yeah." Jason said as he looked around trying to find

her, "You said something about not being who you appear to be."

"I did not say it in those exact words, but yes you are correct."

"I never understood that back then and I don't understand it now." He said, feeling kind of crazy talking to himself. Oubrago, through the mind-link, sensed that Jason was beginning to feel uncomfortable. So she decided to show Jason what she really looked like.

"Well Oubrago?" He asked while noticing something flying across the bright blue, alien, sky.

"Well what, Jason?" She answered, touching him on the shoulder causing him to turn very quickly and nearly stumble over his own two feet.

Standing in front of Jason was a beautiful, bald, orange skinned, humanoid female figure. He knew that this person standing before him was a female, due to certain physical female features. She had a brown leather vest, with what looked like black spandex pants and black, ankle high, leather boots. She had what appeared to be two knives strapped to both of her thighs. The one on the right thigh was longer, with a slightly curved handle.

"Who are you!?!" Said Jason, looking a bit startled.

"It is I, Oubrago." She answered, walking closer toward him. But Jason, who was feeling a little apprehensive, kept backing away.

"You're not Oubrago, I mean you can't be."

"But I am, Jason." She said, placing her hands on her

hips and turning her body around like a fashion model would, "This is what I really look like and this was my planet, my home before the war."

"O.K. It makes sense." Jason said under his breath, desperately trying to understand the situation.

"What does?" She asked, tilting her head to the side in confusion.

"That you're Oubrago."

Jason sat on the same rock as before, except that now he sat on the edge leaving enough space for her to sit beside him. But she didn't, at least not until he gestured that she could. Although he didn't have to, she could sense that he wanted her to sit next to him. But she was being stubborn, just one of the things she learned from observing humans interact with each other.

"Please explain yourself, Jason." She said, finally sitting beside him.

"Well, it's simple." He said, "You're the only one who walked with me into the alley and, you're the only one who's touching the sides of my head. Hell, we're probably the only two out in the snow at this time. Speaking of which, how long have we been doing this for?"

"I am relieved that you believe me, and we have been doing this for approximately five of your Earth minutes."

"It seems longer. But anyway, why did you bring me here and what did you want to show me?"

"I wanted to show you my true identity, not to mention what my planet looked like seven days prior to the invasion." She sadly said.

"Why can't you look like this every day on Earth?"

"Because I, along with a few hundred of my people, are in hiding." Said Oubrago, looking deep into his eyes.

Jason, who couldn't resist looking into her eyes, gets up abruptly from the rock very confused. "I don't understand, what are you hiding from?"

"The Draqkor." She said while getting up from the rock to stand near Jason, who was now closer to the edge of the cliff than before, looking out as far as the eye can see. "They are not what the people of Earth perceive them to be. They are not the peaceful and caring people they have proclaimed themselves to be."

"Then what are they?" He asked as he turned to look at her face, not believing how pretty she really was.

"They are a conquering people." She said, "As you have been taught in school, our solar system is comprised of five planets Draqkorlamaque, Quezok, Korlak, Chabalar and, Drakkorlam." With a wave of her hand, a small three dimensional scale model of a solar system appeared between herself and Jason. As she named each planet, they would inflate and deflate. The planets were circling, counter clockwise, around huge twin Suns that Jason thought made the Sun on Earth look like a marble ball if compared side by side.

"Yeah, our teacher said that the Draqkor couldn't colonize two planets…" He paused for a moment, again noticing something flying in the sky. This time it was a little closer than before. "Chabalar and Drakkorlam. But the teacher, in fact not even the text books explained why."

"I will tell you why." Oubrago said as she looked up at the sky to see what Jason was so intrigued by. "They do not 'Colonize' as your teacher's and text books have taught, they invade and conquer."

The scenery suddenly changed, Jason and Oubrago were no longer on the planet surface, they were now on board a ship in space orbiting a planet which was twenty times larger than Jupiter. There were Draqkor's walking all around them, and outside there were ships of different size and shape preparing for what he assumed was an invasion. However, he quickly dismissed that notion after observing that the ships were facing away from the planet into space.

"Where are we now?" Asked Jason, as he dodged and weaved, trying to stay out of the way from the Draqkor's that were walking around him.

"We are onboard the Draqkorlamaque warship Rorlorad, and just as you assumed, they are preparing for an invasion of a nearby planet which you have learned about, Korlak."

There were Draqkorlamaque aliens everywhere, some were working near their stations and others were walking to and from the bridge. Most of the aliens were passing right through both Oubrago and Jason.

"Wow… This is so cool." Said Jason with great excitement.

"Are you cold Jason? Shall I—"

"No, No Oubrago, I'm fine." He said, cutting off before she could react, "What I meant by using the word cool, is that I find it amazing that the Draqkorlamaque's can walk directly through us as if though we were ghosts or phantoms."

"If you would look out the window Jason, you will notice that we are now in orbit around a smaller planet and the ships are now pointing toward it."

"Is that Korlak?"

"Yes."

Jason then walked toward one of the workstations and waved his hand up and down, in front of the aliens face. He then walked toward a seat which was positioned on the center of the bridge, that he assumed was the captains chair, and did the same thing. Jason, pretending to be the captain, stands in front of the real captain with both hands poised by his hips inhaling his breath causing his chest to look bigger. He then raised his left eyebrow, and shouted, "Fire!" The ship then shot a bolt of energy at the planet. Jason, feeling a little frightened, hurried back to Oubrago's side.

"Tell me that I didn't do that."

"No, you did not." Oubrago assured him.

"But then how, never mind I don't wanna know."

Within moments, every Draqkorlamaque ship was firing on the planet. Small ships, which Jason guessed were escape ships, were speeding by the Draqkorlamaque fleet. The attack ships destroyed a few of the fleeing vessels, but some still managed to get through. However, a majority of the Draqkorlamaque ships followed the Korlak escape vessels, including the ship in which Oubrago and Jason were in. After a few minutes of chasing and destroying several hundred ships, the Draqkor's were forced to retreat back to the planet Korlak, due to the Chabalar attack ships that were rapidly approaching and which outnumbered them twenty to one.

"Yeah baby!!!" Jason yelled, tapping Oubrago on the back of her shoulder in excitement that at least some of the escaped ships made it to safety.

As the Rorlorad once again orbited the planet Korlak, Oubrago looked into Jason's eyes and he for some unknown reason couldn't help but to look into hers. By the time Jason realized what was happening, both he and Oubrago were back on the surface of Drakkorlam and Jason yet again was staring at the flying object.

"Jason, I have noticed your interest in one of my planets wildlife." Said Oubrago.

"Yeah, what the heck is that up there?"

"That is the equivalent to one of your exotic, but almost extinct, birds back on Earth," She said, "It's resemblance is that of a Falcon."

"You know, you're right. It does look like a falcon from this far." Jason raised his left hand to his eyebrow, blocking the Suns glare, to try to get a better view.

"Would you care to see it at a much closer range, Jason?"

"Sure, if it's possible."

Seconds later, the bird landed on the rock that they had both sat on. The bird was much larger than any other bird Jason had ever seen on Earth, it had brown almost rust colored feathers and a red beak with fangs protruding from the sides. The bird stood there, ruffling its feathers and watching the both of them. Every so often it would jerk its head forward and spread its wings, making a loud screeching, almost menacing, sound.

"Why is it making that horrible sound?" Asked Jason, covering his ears.

"The Crisash's, or birds as you would call them, are known for two things." She said while approaching the winged creature, "The first is their physical prowess and the second thing they are known for is that they are very territorial."

"Will it bite me if I touch it?"

"No… At least not this one."

"And why is that?"

"Because this Crisash belongs to me, she is what you would consider a pet. But to me she is no pet, she is a friend, and her name is Sulyse."

"That's so cool." He said, cautiously approaching the bird, "Can I touch it?"

"Yes you may."

Jason walked toward the bird and began to pet it, very gently, on the head with one hand while rubbing its feathery wings with the other. Oubrago and Jason remained with the bird for a long time, watching it fly and hunt. "Oh my gosh! The party!" Jason blurted out.

"Do not worry yourself, Jason. As I have mentioned earlier, although time may appear to go faster here it has only been twenty of your minutes." She told him, "But yes, perhaps we should be returning back to your house for the party."

After Jason said his farewell to Sulyse, Oubrago gave the bird one, long, last hug. He noticed a tear flowing from her eye down her cheek, but he didn't say anything. In a blink of an eye Jason again surrounded by snow, feeling a little cold and disoriented. After a couple of seconds, they both walked out of the alley and headed home. It seemed like a long walk, even though they went home the same way they came. The reason it felt long was due to their silence, none of them spoke a word to each other, at least not until they arrived on the front porch of the house. From outside, they were able to hear the loud music being played.

"Oubrago, before we go in I'd like to thank you."

"Thank me for what Jason?"

"For trusting me with your secret and for showing me what and who the Draqkorlamaque's really are."

"I feel I must caution you not to tell anyone about what I have shown you."

"Why not?"

"Please… Just trust me and say nothing to no one, it would be dangerous for the both of us."

"O.K." He said, raising his right hand, "I promise not to tell a soul."

"Thank you."

"I do have a question for you, though not of the same subject."

"What is it?"

"Why were you crying when you hugged your bird?"

"She was killed, in part by a Draqkorlamaque soldier."

"How?"

"The soldier had me cornered on the edge of the mountain that I showed you, when the soldier fired at me Sulyse flew between myself and the blast, taking the full impact."

"So, she died?"

"No. Not at that moment…" She paused, gathering her composure, "After I killed the soldier, by throwing him over the mountain, I walked toward Sulyse and realized that her injuries were very severe. I did the only thing that was possible, I ended her misery and suffering by killing her."

It was now Jason who was tearing. He waited a few seconds before going inside the house to enjoy Christmas, and his birthday.

CHAPTER – 8

It's late, two hours after Jason's birthday party had ended and nearly everybody is gone. Before they left though, he made certain that he thanked them all for coming to his eighteenth birthday. Although not everyone had gone, Oubrago remained, as she often did, to help his mother clean up. Oubrago would come over to the house so often that the Briggs family had given her the guest bedroom to sleep in, she even had her own set of house keys so that she could come and go as she pleased. Jason, laying down on his bed face up, was alone, lost in thought till someone knocked on his bedroom door.

"Come in." He said, sitting up on the edge of the bed.

"Are you dressed?" The person asked.

Quickly recognizing the voice, Jason sarcastically replied, "I wouldn't tell you to come in if I wasn't Maggie."

"I just wanted to make sure." She said, walking in and closing the door behind her.

Maggie and Jason were in the room for what seemed hours putting his gifts away, folding his clothes and placing them in their proper dresser draws. After putting everything away, they both sat on the bed for awhile, in silence. The silence was suddenly interrupted when Jason grabbed one of two pillows he had on the bed, and hit Maggie on the head. Maggie of course retaliated by grabbing the other pillow and bashing him across the head, knocking him off the bed. They played like that for an hour before falling to the carpeted floor from exhaustion. As soon as they gathered their strength they both helped each other up from the floor and again sat on the bed, in silence. Jason was about to grab the pillow and start the game all over again but Maggie, apparently, had other plans. She grabbed his face gently and gave him a long, passionate, kiss on the lips. He didn't know how to react to what had just happened, other than to get up from the bed and walk over toward the window.

"Maggie, why did you do that?"

"Isn't it obvious Jason."

"Yeah. I mean, no… What is?"

"I know how you feel about me," She said, getting up from the bed to stand by him, "I've always known how you felt about me, ever since we were young. I knew you liked me, but I guess you didn't know that I liked you as well."

"Oh, believe me, I knew. But I wasn't too sure, and was afraid that if I expressed myself to you it would've probably ruin our good friendship."

"Is that why you got up from the bed when I kissed you, because I've ruined our friendship?" She asked, feeling a little guilty and upset.

"No. Of course not," He said, "Don't you even dare think that."

"Then why Jason?" She wanted to know, "Why did

you walk away when I kissed you?"

"I don't know Maggie, I guess I didn't expect that from you." He said, looking at her eyes and she into his.

As they both gazed into each other's eyes, Jason could see that she really liked him, but for some he couldn't tell or even show her how he felt about her. He had other plans, and in those plans he didn't see himself getting emotionally involved with anyone. Maggie sees this by looking in his eyes, but she could also sense a hint of confusion, of not being certain about what he wanted out of life.

"I'll tell you what, Jason. Why don't we try this for awhile and take it one step at a time."

"O.K. I can deal with that."

It was silent in the room and for at least a half hour they both stared out the window before sitting back down on the bed, this time much closer than before.

"Maggie, where do you see yourself in five to ten years from now?" He asked.

"I see myself married to you." She quickly replied.

"No. For real." He said smiling and feeling a bit embarrassed.

"I am being real." She said, "I see myself married to you with two, maybe three kids and a dog, living in a nice two floor house."

"O.K. Please stop, because you almost looked serious when you said that."

"I was." Said Maggie, feeling a little annoyed that Jason didn't take her serious. "What about you Jason, where do you see yourself in five to ten years from now?"

"I see myself in the military, Air/Space Force to be exact, flying one of those new experimental fighter jets I've read about. Living in a nice house, or apartment, with a dog. No kids and not married, at least not during the next five years, perhaps in the following five years after that."

The phone is ringing and they both hear it, but ignore it. They know that either Jason's mother, or father, will answer it. Moments later, Jason's mother knocks on the door and peeks her head in, "Maggie that was your mother on the phone, which by the way Jason she said happy birthday, she asked me to tell you not to go home too late."

"I'm going home right now, thanks for the message Mrs. Briggs"

"Jason why don't you walk her home?" Suggested his mother.

Together they walked out the door, bundled up in their coats and looking like two eight year olds playing with snow. It was late, no one saw them except for Jason's parents who watched from the window till they got as far as the eye can see...

A four man shuttle has just landed on the docking area of the D.C. ship, onboard were Beklota, his two personal guards and, of course, the pilot. Greeting them was the Commander of the D.C. ship, Zard, who urgently requested that Beklota come to his ship first before going on his six month inspection tour of all the Earth based ships, which would begin in

Europe. The shuttle doors opened and a few seconds later the guards, followed by Beklota, exited the shuttle and together walked toward Zard.

"Greetings Beklota." Said Zard as he met them halfway.

"Greetings Zard," He said, gesturing with his hand to the guards to stay behind and mind the shuttle. "What news do you have for me that required my immediate attention."

"If you would accompany me to the nearest Historical Viewing Laboratory I will show you."

"Very well then, proceed." Together they walked out the shuttle-bay, made a right down a poorly lit corridor, where moments later they arrived at their destination.

There are Historical Viewing Laboratories (H.V.L.) on every ship, but none is as large or technologically advanced, other than the Avoloxzia, as the D.C. ship. The D.C. ship collects the information from every Draqkorlamaque ship on Earth, then the scientists prioritize the information and transmits all the data to the Avoloxzia. Zard felt that the data he discovered would be best told in person, and what better way to get a promotion than to give it face to face.

Beklota was now connected to the viewing machine and in seconds his mind was flooded with newspaper reports, television reports, Top Secret Government reports and interviews. All were based on the 1947 crash landing of two unidentified flying objects near Roswell, New Mexico.

"Why did you not follow protocol and forward this information to the Avoloxzia, rather than have me come here?" Asked Beklota, disconnecting himself from the viewing machine.

"I knew you would not get it as quickly and probably not as accurate."

"But I still would have received the data… Correct?"

"Yes, but –"

"There is a human phrase used to describe what you have just done," Beklota said, trying to remember the exact words, "I believe it is called 'Kissing Ass.'"

"Is 'Kissing Ass' a bad thing?"

"That would depend on what you think you have accomplished by giving me this information in person."

"Perhaps a promotion?"

"Ah, yes. Your promotion… I will consider it."

"And what of the information?" Asked Zard most eagerly, "Are we going to use it against the humans?"

"No, not yet. Soon, very soon." Said Beklota as he and Zard walked out from the H.V.L. back to the docking area, "But we must first obtain more evidence."

CHAPTER – 9

2052.

Jason has graduated high school and immediately enlisted in the military service, against his parent's wishes, just as he has always planned since the age of fifteen. He wasn't the only one to join the military, so did Jesus, also disobeying his parents. Both are participating in a five man flying formation training session above Europe's stratosphere, ready to go to space and orbit Earth where they will then land on the docking-bay of the U.S.S. Freedom.

The U.S.S. Freedom is a spacecraft carrier designed from the late twentieth century aircraft carriers, with a minor difference. In the aircraft carriers of the twentieth century, the fighter jets or helicopters landed on the flight deck of the sea ship in which they would then be put in an elevator lift and taken to a lower deck. On the spacecraft carrier's there is no flight deck, the space fighters can either land through the bow or stern sections of the ship.

The space fighters were flying in a standard triangle formation, like migrating ducks. Jason and Jesus would almost always fly alongside each other, so that every once and awhile they can glance at one another when talking.

"You seem awfully quiet over there Jiggy – J." Said

Jason through the comm – system.

Jiggy – J is a nick – name Jason gave Jesus during their senior year of high school, he knew Jesus hated nick – names, but he gave him one anyway. Of course Jason was one of the few people who could call him that, probably the only one who can get away with it.

"No. I was just thinking about something." said Jesus, glancing over at Jason's space fighter.

"Please feel free to tell the class." Jason said jokingly.

"Well, if you really must know, I was actually day-dreaming."

"Liar!"

"To be honest, I was just thinking about my future." He said, sounding a little depressed.

"What about it?"

"Do you think I'll ever get married and have any children?"

"Of course you will."

"Really." he doubted, "Here I am, about a year and a half out of high school, with a military career. When, where and, how, do you suppose am I gonna meet this special some-one?"

"Who knows," He said trying to re-assure him, "you might meet somebody who's in the military, who's probably talking about the same thing to one of her friends. I've seen the way some of the women on the carrier look at you."

"Really, you think so?" Jesus asked, again glancing over at Jason's fighter.

"No. Not really." Jason said, followed by laughter from the both of them.

"Look alive people," The wing commander's voice interrupted through the comm – system, "We're coming up on the U.S.S. Freedom… E.T.A. two minutes."

"Jason, are you still going to propose to Maggie?"

"Yep." Answered Jason, as he searched his flight suit and finding the ring box, "Got the engagement ring right here."

Jesus could see that Jason was holding his arm up, as if holding something that was obviously to small for him to see from their distance, "And when are you planning on doing this?"

"During my shore–leave next month."

Beklota's shuttle has just docked on the Avoloxzia from his six month tour where he is greeted, unannounced, by Zard and his leading scientist on Earth history, Duural. "To what do I owe this visit?" He asked.

"We have found the evidence that we were searching for." Said Zard, very excitingly.

"Well, is this the planet they came to or not?" Beklota asked as they walked out from the docking – bay toward his living quarters.

"Yes…" He hesitated for a moment, "But there is a problem."

"What kind of problem?"

"It would seem that the fugitives did indeed land on

this planet, and yes our soldiers were in pursuit. However, they came to this planet, the North American Continent, during a horrendous summer lightning storm which caused the two ships to be hit by a bolt of lightning and crash land here on Earth."

"Does that mean they died on impact?" Asked Beklota, as he lead the way into his quarters.

"Not quite, sir." Duural interjected, "It would appear that the U.S. Government, upon discovering the alien wreckage and the four out of five survivors, stole the technology and used it to help advance human technology."

"What about the survivors?" A very concerned Beklota asked.

"The pursuing ships' pilot died on impact, however the co-pilot and tactical soldier survived and so did the two Half-breed slaves from the planet Drakkorlam." Duural said. At that point Zard gave Duural a cold look, as if warning him not to speak unless spoken to.

"How long did these survivors live for?" Beklota demanded to know.

"Not long enough, sir." Said Zard.

"Explain."

"Apparently the U.S. Government, as did most governments at that time, took the survivors and proceeded to commit cruel experimentations which eventually killed them."

"Zard, what did you mean by 'As did most governments at that time?. Are you saying that Earth has been visited by other alien species. If so, did they kill them as well?"

"Earth has been visited by other alien species for centuries, but contact has never occurred between the humans and aliens."

"These other species, can we identify any of them?" Beklota asked, looking directly at Duural.

Duural hesitated for a quick second and glanced toward at Zard, who was also looking at him, as if asking permission to answer the question. "No, sir. We have nothing on our data that can identify any of the ships."

"Why did the humans kill our people?" Asked Beklota, turning his attention toward Zard.

"Well sir, the humans of that time believed in the possibility of alien life,
but could not accept it. You must understand that if, at that time, alien life did
exist their religious beliefs and structure would collapse."

"Then it appears that I have no choice but to take back what does not belong to them, by whatever means are necessary, even if it means war."

"We must not let it come to that!" Duural said aloud.

"Why not?"

"Who is to say that these people would not have developed the technology that they have now on their own?"

"I would disagree with Duural's opinion." Said Zard.

"Why is that?"

"Look at their history," Zard said, "Up until the late

eight-teen hundreds, they used horses and coal burning loco-motives for transportation. In the first few years the automo-bile was created and manufactured, but none were as fast as the ones built during the late 1940's. Even their air transportation has advanced from flying in the air to traveling in space, their computers went from being the size of refrigerators to fitting around there wrists. They have even managed to harness the power of the Atom and used it on one another."

Beklota sat in silence for awhile, contemplating on what he should do. He thought about what Duural and Zard had said. But there was one thought that weighed heavily on his mind, and that was on the way his people suffered and died in a horrific manner by human hands. "Beklota to the Bridge," He said, pressing the comm-system located on the armrest of his chair, "Order all of the Draqkorlamaque ships on Earth to return to the Avoloxzia immediately."

One day later. Thirteen hundred hours.

Jason's shift ended three and a half hours ago, he's in his sleeping quarters deeply asleep and having a dream he most likely will not remember till at least the end of the week or unless something happens which will trigger his memory of the dream. He is suddenly awoken by the comm-system calling his name, "Jason Briggs, report to the ships Bridge." He immediately recognized the voice, it was Captain Wilkins.

Captain Wilkins is a bald, well shaved, Afro-American man with a deep voice that sounded like a bullhorn. He is well respected and has always been, since the beginning of his military career when he served on board the sea ship U.S.S. Kennedy, which was now decommissioned.

"I'm on my way sir." Responded Jason, wiping the sleep from his eyes.

As Jason walked toward the Bridge, he tried to figure out what could be so urgent that the Captain himself called for him, normally the Commander or a lower ranking officer would make the call. He was so nervous that as he got close to the Bridge he began to create all sorts of scenarios that would cause the Captain to contact him personally, but he could not think of anything he did wrong and before he knew it he was walking through the Bridge doors.

"There goes another one sir." Said the Commander, referring to a Draqkorlamaque ship.

"How many does that make?" Asked Captain Wilkins.

"I believe that makes five within the last hour."

"What the Hell is going on?" The Captain whispered.

"Jason Briggs reporting as requested, sir." He said, while saluting the Captain.

"As you were pilot." He said, "It would seem that I am the bearer of bad news son. Please come with me to the war room."

Jason followed the Captain to the war room, which was located across the hall from the Bridge. The war room was just as large as the Bridge, without all the technical consoles. The room had all kinds of Earth maps, star-charts, and computer terminals to access military hardware. But in order for the computer terminals to function it needs a numerical code, which only the Captain, the Commander, and the Tactical officer had, there was also a long oval conference table.

"Please, have a seat." The Captain told him, as he also sat down on the swivel chair beside him. "Jason, we've just received word that your father has suffered a heart-attack and is in critical condition at the New York Presbyterian Hospital."

Jason feels a lump begin to build in his throat and his eyes start to water, but he holds his composure so as not to let a tear out. The Captain, however, notices and says, "It's alright Jason, only the strongest and bravest of men cry." As soon as it was said, Jason bursts into tears.

The Captain lets Jason grieve for a few minutes, "Jason, I'm granting you a one month emergency shore leave on top of your next month's week long shore leave." He said, getting up from the chair to comfort Jason who was wiping the tears from his eyes. "You are to report to the flight deck, where there will be a shuttle ready to escort you to New York."

"May I have a few minutes to gather some of my things from my sleeping quarters."

"Sure son, take as long as you need." He said, "Oh, and pilot. Be strong and keep your chin up, everything's going to be alright."

CHAPTER – 10

Jason has just arrived at the hospital and is greeted by his mother who was sitting down in the waiting area, along with several other people that were also waiting for either a family member or a doctor. "Mom, how did this happen to dad?" He asked, worried and concerned for his fathers well being.

"First take a deep breath and relax." She told him, as she got up from the chair and put her arms around him with tears flowing from her eyes. He hugged her as tight as he could and tried to relax, but he could not, he just kept crying uncontrollably.

Sandra led Jason toward two empty chairs near the receptionist desk, "You know how your father gets when he goes to the attic." She said, wiping her tears, "He began to move things around, looking for something or another, I don't quite remember what it was. Before I realized it, he was cleaning the entire attic alone. That's when I heard a loud thumping sound, as if though something heavy had dropped. When I went to check what it was, I saw your father on the floor clenching his chest."

Jason stood quiet for awhile, observing the many doctors and nurses walking about. Some were caring to patients needs and others were talking to the patients family. He noticed that some of them were happy to talk to doctors and nurses, but he also noticed that some had a sad almost sorrow look on their face, most of which were crying. However, he could not tell if they were tears of joy or pain.

"Mom how long have the doctors been with dad?" Asked Jason, hoping that when the doctors do come they would have good news.

"At least an hour and a half."

About twenty-five minutes later, Maggie, his Aunt Natasha and, Oubrago, walk up toward the receptionist desk at which point the receptionist directs them to where Jason and Sandra were seated.

"How is he?" Natasha asked, hugging Sandra gently.

"I don't know." She answered, getting a little more worried, "The doctors said they would let me know as soon as possible."

As Sandra begins to explain to Natasha, Maggie and Oubrago what happened to her husband, Jason is thinking of a way to try and help the situation, but he realizes that there is nothing he can do. His mothers explanation was close to an end, and he looks at all three of them when it suddenly occurs to him that the solution to his fathers problem was right in front of him all along, "Oubrago."

"Yes Jason?" She responded.

"What?" He said, not realizing that he, once again, was thinking out loud.

"You said my name."

"No I didn't. I mean yeah… Can I speak to you for a

minute?" He asked, as he got up from the chair.

Oubrago agrees and walks with Jason, who was unusually quiet. She knew he had a lot on his mind and, she figured that, he asked her to walk with him so that he can let some of it out. But she was wrong, he did not ask her to walk with him so that he can let his feelings be known to her, he had an idea, one that could help his father. Jason took Oubrago to the hospital lobby and, for a few seconds, they watched two E.M.T.'s bring in a patient who had a kitchen knife embedded in the chest. There was blood on the patient, as well as on both of the E.M.T.'s. but what amazed Jason and Oubrago wasn't the blood, it was the patient, who was alive and well aware of his condition. The patient was speaking to the E.M.T.'s in such a calm manner, that it made Jason wonder if the patient actually knew what was sticking out of his torso.

"Oubrago." Said Jason, still staring at the patient, "Can you help my father?"

"What do you mean?" Oubrago asked.

"I mean can you help him the way you've helped me. Ever since the day I came home from school with the flu, which you cured me of, I have never again gotten sick, broken or fractured a bone. So again, I'm asking you, no I'm begging you, can you help my father?"

"No." She said, looking into his eyes.

"What do you mean, no?" Surprised at the answer.

"I can not help your father."

"Why not!?!"

"Due to the bond we share."

"Bond, what bond?" He curiously asked.

"You and I, since the day of the flu, now share a bond." She said, "A genetic bond, which in its most simplest terms is a mixture of both of our D.N.A."

"A genetic bond?" He said in doubt, "So let me get this straight. What you're trying to tell me is that we now have the same blood type or something."

"Not entirely true." She began to explain, "You have to understand. Once someone from my species genetically bonds with another, they cannot do anything another being of the same species, or for that matter any other species. Think of it as a good, long lasting, marriage."

"So what you're saying is 'Til' death do us part.'" Said Jason, trying to make a joke out of it.

"In a matter of speaking, yes." She answered, very seriously.

It was a quiet walk back to the waiting room, where Sandra and Maggie were
now talking to a doctor. "John will have to remain in the hospital for a few days for further observations even though he seems to be fine at this time." Said Doctor Leon.

Doctor Leon is one of the chief surgeons of the hospital, he is a tall man in his early fifties with thicker than thin glasses, huge hands, and a receding hairline.

"Can we see him?" Sandra asked, concerned but relieved that her husband was alive.

"Yes of course." Dr. Leon said, leading the way to

the elevator that would take them to the floor in which her husband's room is located.

Johns room was on the fifth floor to the rear of the hospital, from their they had a wonderful, almost perfect, view of the Hudson River. The river was gleaming brightly from the suns ray's, Jason was watching the Circle Line coming from one side of the river and a tugboat coming from the other, while the family and doctor were standing near the bed. Since entering the room he hasn't once looked at his father, who was connected to a heart monitor. He just walked past his father's bed directly to the window, not so much as a glimpse from his part was given toward the hospital bed.

"Now please try not to let Mr. Briggs talk much, he is exhausted and must get plenty of rest." Said Dr. Leon, "Don't misunderstand me, he can talk. But he might not be able to say full sentence's, at least not right away."

John was conscience while the doctor was talking, he's been awake since they entered the room. He saw when Jason walked in and went straight toward the window, he could tell something was bothering him just by his facial expression. It was quiet long after the doctor left, it was as if though no one wanted to say anything so that John won't feel like he had to say something. However, John would be the first to break the silence.

"Jason." He whispered, sounding almost hoarse and tapping the edge of the bed gently, hoping that he would sit next to him.

"John, honey you –" Sandra was cut off when John

placed his finger on his lips and shushed her.

It took Jason a few seconds to convince himself to sit next to his father, who turned on the H.3-D.T.V. which mounted on a shelf on the corner of the room. He rubbed his hands across Jason's back, letting him know that he was feeling better. Jason couldn't hold his emotion in any longer, he hugged his father tight, and began to cry uncontrollably.

"It's O.K. Jason, I'm alright now." John said, assuring him that he was alive and wasn't planning on going anywhere just yet.

Several minutes of silence passes and a television special report comes on, at that same moment Oubrago excuses herself from the room.

"Good afternoon, this is Chris Turner with some urgent news." He said, "It would appear that our good friends, the Draqkor, are leaving. Alexandra Booth is out on the field with further news."

Surprised, John looked at Jason, "I guess I was wrong son, they were sincere
when they said that they came in peace." He said, as they continued to look at the news.
***
"Oubrago, can you hear me?" Asked the voice.

"Give me a second." Responded Oubrago, as she walked into one of the hospital's supply rooms.

Oubrago was receiving the message from one of the operatives stationed on the mother-ship. The operative, just like Oubrago, must not be seen communicating the way they were, which was through Mind-Link-Telepathy (M.L.T.). The M.L.T. works much like the mind-link that Oubrago shared with Jason, except that with the M.L.T. there doesn't have to be any genetic physical bond between the communicating parties, which can be more than two communicators.

"Go on Duural." She said.

"The Draqkor are withdrawing from Earth, they have ordered every Draqkor to report to their ships for immediate rendezvous with the Avoloxzia." Duural said.

"Then it is safe to assume that they have found the ships they were searching for?"

"No." He said, "Not quite."

"I do not understand Duural, please explain."

"It would seem that the people of Earth, during 1947, encountered two unidentified flying objects which crashed in New Mexico near a small town called Roswell. The incident was quickly concealed from the public by the government, but not quick enough, the public eventually found out and was not told of the truth until the year 2018. However, what the humans were not aware of was the fact that there were four alien survivors who were severely tortured and killed."

"What are the Draqkor planning on doing?"

"Is it not obvious?." Duural said, "They are preparing for an invasion."

The Briggs family are watching the H.3-D.T.V. as Oubrago walks back into the room. Jason looks at her, as if waiting for an explanation, but he doesn't get one. At least not there, at that precise moment.

"Jason." Said Oubrago, "May I have a word with you in private."

"Yeah, sure." He said, following Oubrago out the door.

They walked together, in silence, looking for a secluded area. After a few minutes, she leads him into the supply room she had received the M.L.T.

"I know what you're going to say." He said.

"Do you, now." She said, "I did not know humans had evolved during the last couple of years, to read minds."

"Well aren't we sarcastic. What I meant was, I know you have to leave and report back to the mother-ship."

"No Jason. That is not what I was going to say…" Oubrago tells Jason about the message she received, which took awhile to explain, and when all was said and done he still didn't understand. She repeated herself again, this time much slower.

"–But don't they understand that the humans of the past were ignorant to things they couldn't explain." Said Jason.

"No, they do not." She said, "For they are ignorant in there own way."

"Now what happens, Oubrago?"

"Now I must give you what you were destined to have."

Oubrago walks closer toward Jason, places her fingers on the side of his temples, and begins to transfer both knowledge and the use of certain abilities such as telekinesis, telepathy, which he had already experienced, and the ability to project waves and bolts of energy from his hands. Jason, having the trust he did for Oubrago, did not feel the slightest bit scared or nervous. After seven seconds, she took her fingers away from his temples and was done. Jason felt as if though he were a new person who has just had a ton lifted from his shoulder, full of energy. They both head back to the room, again in silence. When they arrive to the room, there was a fighter pilot waiting for Jason.

"Private Briggs." The fighter pilot said, "I have orders to escort you back to the
U.S.S. Freedom, with the Captain's deepest apologies." The fighter pilot was a tall Hispanic man with huge broad shoulders, short hair and a clean-shaved face.

"Can you give me a couple of minutes to say goodbye to my family?" Asked Jason.

"Of course." Said the pilot, as he marched out the door and stood there with his arms folded behind him.

"Jason, do you know what's going on?" John asked.

"No." Answered Jason, lying to his father for the first time. He then hugged him, and wished him well. He then did the same to his mother, his aunt, Maggie, Oubrago, and again his father, quickly wiping his tears before leaving with his escort.

CHAPTER – 11

One hour later.

World leaders and representatives from every nation on Earth have gathered in the United Nations, and are discussing the sudden departure of several Draqkorlamaque ships.

"People, we have a very serious situation." Said the Prime Minister of England, Sir. Andrew Blake, "No matter how many times we have tried to re-establish communication with the Draqkorlamaque's, particularly Beklota, we get no response."

"Do you think they have discovered what they were searching for?" Asked Nikita Borishnovka, first female President of the Soviet Union.

"Even if they did, why are they reacting in this way?" Chinese Ambassador,

Chow Tso Li, asked.

"Let's be serious." The President of the United States, James K. Williams, said. He was the second Afro-American to be elected President, the first being a woman. "It's no longer a secret, so stop pretending as if you don't already know."

"Know what? Mr. President." Chow Tso Li asked, but was ignored.

"You are correct of that situation, and what I mean

is that the people of that time who chose to cover-up the incident had no choice in making their decision." Said the Russian President.

"Cover what up?" The Chinese Ambassador wanted to know, "What decision?"

"Ambassador, I'm certain you've heard about the Roswell Incident of 1947. I mean it's no secret, not anymore." Said President Williams as he stood up from his chair and walked to the podium and began to speak a little louder, even though there was a microphone. "What I am about to say has only been known to the leaders and rulers of the following countries, the U.S., the Soviet Union, England, China, Japan, and Germany. The fact, as you all know, is that two alien space craft's did crash near a small town called Roswell in 1947. Another fact, people have witnessed this incident and many others, before and after the famous incident. But what is not known to the public is that the leaders and rulers of the previously mentioned countries came together, in secrecy, to discuss the procedure should another incident occur. This newly formed procedure called for the execution of any and all alien life forms, if possible. Fortunately we have only had to do that twice, once in the U.S. and the other in the Soviet Union."

"What about the wreckage that was also discovered and witnessed to be unbreakable?" The Ambassador asked.

President Williams ignored the question, and walked back to the desk from which he came. When he got to the desk he reached over, grabbed his briefcase, and with that the meeting was adjourn, or so he assumed. He did not know that the Ambassador was persistent, nor did he notice that he was following him.

"Mr. President! Mr. President!" The Ambassador shouted, as the President finally stopped. "Can I have a minute of your time!?!"

"A minute is all I can spare Mr. Ambassador." The President said, looking at his wristwatch.

"Yes of course." He said while composing himself, "I want to know why my question went unanswered? What are you trying to hide?"

"I'm not trying to hide anything." He said out loud, realizing he was shouting he quickly lowered his voice, "Or rather, we're not trying to hide anything."

"My apologies Mr. President. I did not mean to imply—"

"Come, walk with me Mr. Ambassador." He said, cutting him off in mid-sentence.

The Ambassador followed the President outside the United Nations building and into the back of the security guarded limousine. Once inside, the conversation continued.

"What did you mean by 'We're not trying to hide anything'?" Asked the Ambassador, while getting comfortable.

"You know as well as I do that ever since the world peace, every and all secrets the governments of the world were concealing is now open to the public."

"Yes, of course I know that, it's part of history."

"But what is not part of the history that the public is

not familiar with, is the fact that the world leaders, just as they did immediately after the Roswell Incident, met yet again in Top Secret. This time the topic was to conceal what I consider to be mankind's greatest shame and humiliation."

"I do not understand, I have never heard of this so called 'Top Secret' meeting." Said a confused Ambassador.

"Of course not, only Presidents, Prime Ministers, Dictators, and Royalty, had the proper clearance to know." He said, "Now as I was saying, mankind was a shame at what had happened in the past. You see the people of that time period used the technology to better advance themselves, or should I say ourselves."

"Used. Don't you mean stole." The Ambassador said rather frankly.

"Whatever word you prefer to use, will be fine." Said President Williams as he looked at him with a cold empty stare.

"In what way was the technology used." He said, feeling a little uncomfortable from the Presidents silent stare.

"Okay, here's something to think about." Said the President, leaning forward so no one could hear what he was about to say, even though he knew it was just the two of them, "Before the incident at Roswell, human technology was at a low, there weren't that many 'Head turning' inventions. However, after the incident, technology sky rocketed to the Moon, and I mean that literally. You have to understand that although Russia made it to space first we, the United States, went to the Moon based on the alien technology that yes, we stole. Here is something else to bear in mind, not only has that technology helped us advance into space but look at all the medical breakthroughs that has occurred, such as laser surgery, heart transplants, and the regeneration of limbs derived from stem cell cloning, etc. Here's yet another thing to think about, computers during the 1940's were slow and as large as refrigerators. Hell, a person couldn't have one in his or her apartment because the computer was too big and expensive, but now computers are inexpensive and they also fit in your back pocket. So you see just as I mentioned earlier, we didn't steal anything, we simply borrowed and used it to better advance ourselves."

The President leaned back and, just for a few seconds, it was quiet in the limousine. Ambassador Chow Tso Li was in shock at what he was just told, he knew he couldn't tell anybody because no one would believe him. Then he began to think about all the technological advances the human race had been through, but the thought was quickly interrupted by one of the President's secret service agents. The agent knocked softly on the limousine's, bulletproof, glass window. President Williams, of course, lowered the window halfway.

"Mr. President." The agent said, bending down to the Presidents' eye level, "It seems the Draqkorlamaque mothership has moved away from Earth's orbit, but has dispatched smaller vessels which are orbiting Earth. That's not all Sir, some of these vessels have been flying at close proximity of the spacecraft carriers."

"Have the other world leaders been notified?" A

concerned President asked.

"Yes sir. They're being told now as we speak."

"Mr. Ambassador if you'll excuse me, I--"

"Not a problem Mr. President." Said the Ambassador while opening the limousine door, "Have a pleasant day sir."

President Williams wasted no time, he reached for the car phone which connected him directly to the World Military Council. "General." He said, "Order our space craft carriers to be on full alert." The President then looked up at the clear blue sky and whispered to himself, "My God, what have we done?"

Two hours later.

The fighter pilots of the U.S.S. Freedom have been summoned to the docking-bay, where Captain Wilkins is briefing the pilots on how to operate the newly developed spacecraft's. The spacecraft's were very different than the space fighters they were navigating before, the new crafts were similar to the Stealth B-2 Bomber developed during the 1990's but much smaller and sleeker. It was triangular in shape, with no sharp edges. It had a hump in the front/center, which appeared to be the cockpit. They were metallic black instead of gray, with a certain smoothness to its design, like there former fighters.

"You all have been chosen as the best fighter pilots of the U.S.S. Freedom," Shouted the Captain, who was standing on top of the wing from one of the spacecraft's. "And as the best you will pilot the best fighter crafts technology has to offer."

He paused for a few seconds, so that the pilots could feel good about themselves, before continuing, "As you may or may not know, these space craft's were developed in conjunction with the Draqkor. Meaning that no human, other than the developers, have seen these fighter, nor have they've been tested before. The reason they have never been tested, is due to the fact that they are programmed to genetically bond with the individual pilot. The instant you put on your helmet, the space fighters will bond with you. It will then respond to either voice commands and/or neural interface, the choice is entirely yours. However, I feel that I should warn you that if the fighter craft senses that it, or you, are in danger it will override your commands and try to protect both you and itself."

Jason remembers reading about these space fighters before they were built, during their production stage, back when he was in school. But what he had read sounded nothing like what the Captain said, nor did it describe the way they looked.

"Before I step down from this fighter, do any of you have any questions?" Asked Capt. Wilkins. The docking-bay was silent for a few seconds and, as he hopped off the fighters wing he said, "Good. I'll leave you now so you can get familiar with your fighters."

"This should be interesting." Muttered the Commander loud enough so that only the Captain could hear, as they both walked alongside each other toward the docking-bay entrance.

"Indeed." Responded the Captain.

They both stood there and watched the pilots walk around, under and, on top of the fighters, but none of them, the Captain noticed and expected, has boarded them. After awhile he walked back to the center of the docking-bay, stroking his chin in amusement.

"Navigators." Capt. Wilkins said out loud, again standing on top of one of the fighters, "From the moment you came in contact with the space fighters, as all of you have, you immediately bonded at a genetic level bringing together the gap between man and technology. All you have to do to board the fighters is stand underneath the cockpit, which are the humps located in front of them and it will automatically lower the seat for you." When Capt. Wilkins again stepped down from one of the fighters, the pilots began to board, and the fighters responded just as he said they would.

"WELCOME ABOARD NAVIGATOR JASON BRIGGS." Said the voice of the space fighters' onboard computer. It had a deep, synthesized, masculine voice.

"Thank you, I think." A startled Jason said, "What can I call you?"

"YOU MAY CALL ME AS YOU WISH." The computer answered.

"As I wish, huh?" Jason said, while putting his helmet on, "Chrisash… Do you know what that word means?"

"YES. IT IS A SPECIES OF BIRD FOUND ON THE ONCE PRISON WORLD OF THE HALF-BREEDS, DRAKKORLAM."

"Navigators, you have several hours to get better acquainted to your new space fighters. Enjoy them." Said the Captain aloud before he and the Commander walked out the docking-bay.

"Chrisash." Jason said, "That's what I'm going to call you."

"CHRISASH IS A SUITABLE NAME." The computer replied.

All the space fighters began to depart from the docking-bay, Jason and his fighter were part of the seventh squad to depart. He and Jesus were once again flying side by side, although they could not see each other unless they had their helmets on. The helmets not only acted as a neural interface, but they were the only way the pilots could see out their cockpit. The cockpits, since there was no light coming in from the outside, would be dark if not for the illuminating lights that came from the navigational computers. Every fighter pilot was now flying around the U.S.S. Freedom practicing different maneuvers and formations, and both Jesus and Jason compared notes and showed off their piloting skills for the next few hours…

CHAPTER – 12

Shanstraklar, capitol city of the Draqkorlamaque home world, it is the oldest and most prestigious city in the world. Only high command government officials, scientists, and top ranking Enforcers live in the city. The city was designed and built over five thousand centuries ago by the first ruler of Draqkorlamaque, Pethrasha.

Throughout the city there are statues of the ancient ruler, some made of rare stones and others made of silver. But the largest and most detailed statue, which is made of gold and homage to the great ruler, was erected in the center of the city. The statue is over four hundred stories high and stands, with its legs slightly apart from each other, on a rectangular shaped base which is approximately six hundred feet wide and one hundred stories high, also made of gold. The golden statue stands proudly holding the head of a Quezokorian in one hand, while in the other hand he held the Quezokorian army on his palm.

Pethrasha's reign lasted a century after both the city and statue were built, it is believed among the Draqkorlamaque people that the body of Pethrasha is sealed within the base of the statue, that his blood was drained from his body and courses through the artificial veins of the golden statue.

THE DAY THEY MADE CONTACT

It is nighttime in the ancient city, not many Draqkor people stop to look up and appreciate the two Moons which are also inhabited by Draqkor's. There is a building on the northern section of the ancient city, its purpose is to collect data from off world ships. Shanstraklar government officials have been waiting for Beklota to send them the information, in regards to the two crashed ships.

Inside the building, working on one of the computer terminals, is a Drakkorlam spy posing, holographically, as a Draqkor. The spy has been waiting to intercept the information for many months, ever since another spy serving onboard the Avoloxzia, informed the Drakkorlam home world of the possibility that the Draqkor's were getting close to the discovery of the two ships that crash landed on Earth.

The data is being received on the computer terminal from which the spy is working on, the first thing he does is cover his tracks by making certain that no other terminal can receive the data, the second thing he does is download the data into his Microscopic Optical Computer. The Microscopic Optical Computer is a neural receiver that enables the host to download data from practically any computer terminal through the optical lenses of his or hers eyes. The data is then stored in the microchip, which is surgically implanted in the host's brain. Finally, after successfully downloading the data, he must delete the information from the Draqkor data base.

"You there." Said a Draqkor scientist, "What are you doing? You are not authorized to delete any information. Please step away from the computer terminal."

CHAPTER – 12

"My apologies." Said the spy, while stepping away to allow the scientist to try and fix his mistake, "I am new at this, I did not know that I was deleting the data. I assumed I was saving it."

"Fortunately, you did not yet delete the backup file."

"Only because you interrupted me."

"What!?!"

A physical struggle has now begun between the Drakkorlam spy and the Draqkorlamaque scientist. The spy gives the scientist an uppercut, but the scientist blocks and counteracts with a punch to the spy's stomach, causing him to fall on the floor and catch his breath, also damaging the holographic device and revealing his true identity. The spy had underestimated the fighting skills of the Draqkor scientist, and his intelligence report of them. The scientist turned his back on his opponent, sounded the alarm, and continued to undo the damage caused by the infiltrator.

Seizing the opportunity, the spy quickly stands up, grabs the Draqkor by the back of the head and bashes it through the computer terminal screen. At that same moment, five Draqkorlamaque Enforcers arrive with blasters in hand, quickly shooting energy blasts at the intruder. The spy takes cover behind a pillar to gather his thoughts for an escape, it was obvious he couldn't leave from the same way he entered, instead he makes his own way out. A few of the Enforcer's energy blasts had already softened the wall directly in front of him, all he had to do was run and break through it. However, it wasn't as simple as it seemed, first he had to get rid of a couple of Enforcers.

He takes a few deep breaths, clenches his fists, and comes out from behind the pillar firing bolts of energy from his clenched fists. He manages to hit three out of the five Draqkor Enforcers, but isn't certain whether they're dead or not, and he doesn't intend to stick around to find out either. He turns around and makes a run for the wall while firing a few bolts of energy into the wall, in case it was still too hard.

After breaking through the wall, he runs toward the western section of the city, which happens to be one of the most crowded places of the city. He knows that he will be spotted, due to the fact that he's the only Drakkorlam on the planet, but that is the least of his problems. He still has to avoid being seen by any of the Draqkor Enforcers, which he knows will be patrolling the area in great numbers.

The Drakkorlam spy, while walking and trying to get his holographic disguise to function, knows that he must escape from this planet the hard way. The only possible way to do that is to make it to the Draqkorlamaque space dock, which is located near the end of the city, without being seen, and make it there alive.

Making out of the planet alive shouldn't be hard, seeing as how it's part of his survival instincts. However, since he is a Drakkorlam, making it there without being spotted is proving to be quite difficult. It is so crowded in the western side of the city, that the Draqkor people are constantly rubbing shoulders with each other when walking. While dodging and weaving Draqkor pedestrians he gets bumped hard on the shoulder, as if being provoked to fight. He clenches his fists and is about to show this Draqkor who to bump and who not to bump, when he is suddenly seen by two Enforcers and are coming toward his direction.

He quickly realizes he has no time to make a scene that would most likely get him killed, not by the Draqkor standing in front of him, but by the Enforcers. He tries to blend in with a passing crowd by slipping between them, to avoid being seen. After halfway through the night he finally makes it to the space dock and, as much to his surprise, there's hardly any Enforcers on guard. As far as he can tell there are two on the ground floor guarding the front entrance, four on the roof and probably five, more or less, he thinks, inside.

"I surrender!" Yelled the Drakkorlam spy, as he walked every calmly toward the ground floor Enforcers, "I give up!"

The ground Enforcers, with blasters drawn, approach him very cautiously. When they get within three feet, the spy lets loose a barrage of fire power from his clenched fists, instantly killing the Enforcers. He then runs very quickly inside, before the Enforcers on the roof notice the two dead bodies on the ground. Once inside he sees eleven, instead of the five he had assumed would be on guard, he made certain to be careful and not to be seen as he checked nearly every space craft.

He was unsuccessful in getting inside any of the fast or heavily armed ships, instead he would have to settle for a one man scout-ship. They were built much smaller than a

Draqkorlamaque military craft, they are eight feet long, and five feet wide. They have an oval, almost saucer, shape to them. The scout-ships were built with armament to defend itself, but nothing major, just two small cannons on both the bow and stern sections. Upon boarding and starting the nearly silent engines of the scout-ship, he notices the eleven Enforcers running outside. He figured that one of them, most likely, discovered the two bodies outside.

The spy navigates the scout-ship upward, toward the closed docking-bay doors, not expecting them to be opened he blasts his way through and flies out into space, where he is to meet with another Drakkorlam and pass the information to him or her. As he reaches the Draqkorlamaque stratosphere, he begins to recall the events that transpired on this evening and concludes that this was all too simple.

Unknown to the Drakkorlam spy is the fact that he was right, it was simple. Everything that occurred thus far was choreographed by the Draqkorlamaque Enforcers, from the moment he tried to delete the data to the bump on the shoulder, even in picking the scout-ship he was now navigating. He is also unaware that two of the heavily armed spacecraft's that were docked had pilots already sitting on them, ready to pursue him with orders not to engage until contact was made with his accomplice.

CHAPTER – 13

Hostile is the best way to describe the actions of what appeared to be Draqkorlamaque attack ships, which are flying very close and erratic to the U.S.S. Freedom and other spacecraft carrier's. They were flying so close that the U.S.S. Freedom has recalled all its pilots, who were learning how to navigate their new ships, to return. Even on Earth, above every continent and city, the large ships were replaced by thousand's of the attack vessels flying at close proximity to buildings and commercial airline's.

"Why do you think they're behaving so weird all of a sudden Jason?" Jesus asked, as they both watched the other fighters dock.

"I don't know." Answered Jason, "But I wish I did."

"Jason Briggs. Please report to the Captain's quarters." Said a voice over the

"On my way." Replied Jason, speaking from his personal comm-system.

"I guess I'll see you later Jason." Jesus said, patting Jason on the shoulder and walking in opposite direction.

"Later Jiggy-J."

***

THE DAY THEY MADE CONTACT

The Captain is alone in his quarters with the lights off, in the dark, nobody would even know he was there if it weren't for the illuminating light coming from the stars. For the last couple of hours he's been looking out his window, located on the stern/portside section of the U.S.S. Freedom, watching Draqkor ships get closer and closer to his spacecraft carrier with thousands more going in and out from Earth, wondering what occurred to cause the sudden change between alien and human relations. But that is just one of the things that's on his mind, the other has to do with one of his fighter pilots.

Jason arrives at the Captains' quarters door and knocks, "Come in." Says Captain Wilkins. He walks in and shuts the door behind him very gently, he sees the Captain standing by the window with his hands crossed.

"At ease pilot." The Captain said, "Please feel free to either sit down or
stand by my side, and help in trying to make sense of the sudden change in behavior
made by the Draqkorlamaque."

Jason decides to stand next to the Captain and watch the different alien ships fly by, and around, the U.S.S. Freedom. He then looked at Earth, its continents and oceans, noticing a shimmering light from the corner of his eye he suddenly sees hundreds of thousands of ships, like a swarm of insects, flying towards it.

"You wanted to see me Captain?"

"Yes Jason, I did." He said, turning his attention toward Jason. "It would seem that once again fate has chosen me to be the bearer of bad news. We've just received a message from Earth's New York Presbyterian Hospital, stating that your father has passed away." There was silence for a few seconds in the Captains quarters before he continued, "I am therefore authorizing a seventy-two hour shore-leave to you, to be by your mother's side in this time of need. However, due to the current situation, I cannot provide you with an escort to Earth. Also, as of this moment, you are on emergency standby. Is that clear?."

"Yes sir." Jason said, trying to hold back his emotions.

"Go, get on your fighter." Said the Captain, again looking out the window, "I have already cleared you for take-off."

Jason began to walk out the door when suddenly the Captain calls him, "Jason."

"Yes Captain?"

"I want you to think about something on the way to Earth."

"Think about what Captain?"

"Death."

"What about it?" Asked a confused Jason.

"Death must be a beautiful thing."

"And why is that, sir?"

"Because nobody ever comes back to tell you about it."

He walks out the door and, after a few minutes, the Captain spots Jason's fighter fly towards Earth. He follows it for as far as the eye can see, before once again turning his attention to the Draqkor…

Captain Wilkins felt no need to send an escort with Jason, instead he sent a message to one of the flight deck crewmen to tell him to take his fighter to an old abandoned heliport several blocks away from the hospital.

"This must be the place they told me about before I left." Jason said, while hovering the fighter from one side of the heliport to the other.

The heliport looked old and rundown. There were steel and wooden beams almost everywhere, and an old shack which he assumed used to be either an office or waiting area. As he swooped from side to side, trying to find a suitable place to land, he notices two Draqkorlamaque ships. One of them kept flying around in a circle like a hawk watching its prey, while the other hovered over the Hudson river looking directly at his direction. Jason, after moving a couple of old debris with his landing gear, finds a faded design on the ground with a white circle and the capital letter 'H' in the center.

"Chrisash, if these or any other Draqkorlamaque ship get any closer, I want you to contact me. Understand." Jason said as he took off his head gear, and began to disarm himself.

"UNDERSTOOD." Responded the ship, "BUT ARE YOU CERTAIN YOU SHOULD LEAVE YOUR WEAPON BEHIND?"

"There's no need for it. Besides, I won't be able to enter the hospital without checking my weapon and leaving it with the security guard." He stepped out of his fighter from the top of the cockpit, jumped down, and walked out the gated fence.

Jason made a right when he got to the corner of York Avenue and walked uptown, toward the hospital where he watched a group of Draqkor's, about ten or twelve of them, walking in his direction. As the group passed him he noticed yet another group, across the street on his left side, walking downtown, it was as if they were patrolling the area. He thought he was being paranoid, until he noticed that people were avoiding these groups of Draqkor's. Whenever people saw a group of them, they would either cross the street or get against the wall, it was as if though they feared them. Although, for some reason, Jason didn't fear them, he kept walking, keeping his pace and sometimes walking straight through the alien groups that he seemed to come across every other block.

Jason suddenly gets a beep coming from his comm-system, it's from his fighter, "Yes Chrisash?" He answered, while beginning to turn around and head back to his fighter.

"YOU TOLD ME TO NOTIFY YOU IF ANY SHIP GOT NEAR ME."

"Yeah, well?"

"BE AWARE THAT THE ONE THAT WAS CIRCLING US AS WE LANDED, IS NOW CIRCLING YOU."

Jason looked up, covering the glare of the Sun from his eyes to see the ship, "Got it." He said, "Thanks Chrisash."

"YOU SHOULD ALSO BE AWARE THAT I AM MONITORING YOU AND IF YOU ARE IN ANY DANGER I WILL COME TO YOUR AID. EVEN IF YOU ARE NOT IN DANGER ALL YOU HAVE TO DO IS CONTACT ME AND I WILL ARRIVE IN A MATTER OF MINUTES."

"That's good to know, thanks for that information."

After nearly twenty minutes, Jason walks into the hospital and is greeted by his grieving mother and aunt. His mother hugged him gently, with tears streaming down her cheeks, "He died peacefully in his sleep." She told him. Jason then began to feel a lump in his throat, but he kept his emotions well hidden by not shedding a tear and remaining strong as if in disbelief that his father is dead. He had this numb feeling all over his body, while at the same time feeling a cold chill going up his spine.

"Where is he mom?"

"He's in the hospital's morgue." She said, wiping the tears from her eyes.

"When can we see him?"

"We can view his body tomorrow." She noticed the look of disappointment on
his face almost immediately, "There was nothing you, or anyone else could've done." She gently palmed his cheeks and walked to her sister.

"She is correct, Jason." Said a familiar voice.

"Oubrago?" He heard the voice in his head and answered telepathically, while at the same time trying to find her, "Where are you?"

"I am near." She answered, "I am also pleased that you have learned how to answer me telepathically."

"I have no choice." Jason said, grabbing a magazine and sitting down on one of the many comfort seats in the waiting area.

"Please elaborate?"

"Because I would look like an idiot responding to you verbally, when I could just answer you mentally without anyone noticing."

"Can you sense where I am?"

"Yes, you're entering the hospital… Right about now."

"Very good." Oubrago enters the hospital and gives her condolences to his

mother and her sister who were signing hospital forms, then takes a seat next to

Jason.

To all the people walking by them, it would seem like they were two strangers who didn't know each other, but to the family members, it just seemed like Jason, although looking at a magazine, was mourning his father's death and Oubrago was sitting beside him for comfort. Unaware to anyone, they are actually communicating with each other mentally.

"How are you coping with your fathers death?"

"I'm alright, I guess."

"You, who has not shed a tear, are alright?" She

doubted.

"Yes. I am." He assured her, "Now would you stop asking me."

"Very well then."

For the next ten minutes nothing was said, not verbally nor mentally, at least not by them.

"Jason, Oubrago." Sandra said, "We're going home now."

"Mom I'm afraid I'll have to meet you their."

"Why?"

"Cause, I wasn't escorted here. I flew down in my fighter, which is docked on the old abandoned heliport, several blocks down."

"Then I assume you'll be leaving as soon as possible?"

"No." He said, "However, I'll have to land it on the backyard, but don't
worry, it won't mess up the grass or nothing because it actually hovers."

"O.K. So we'll meet you at the house. Fly carefully." She told him.

CHAPTER – 14

As the scout-ship flew out of the Shanstraklar docking-bay, so too did two Draqkor navigators piloting two heavily armed vessels, they took off immediately after the Drakkorlam spy was well underway. The navigators, Razaal and Commander Katrelk, were ordered not to intercept until contact was made with the accomplice. Unknown to the spy, the Draqkorlamaque vessels are just beyond the scout-ships' long-range scanners.

"Remember Razaal, do not fire until contact has been confirmed. Is that understood?"

"Understood, Commander Katrelk."

The Drakkorlam spy, after three hours, finally arrives at the rendezvous point. But he doesn't see, nor do his scanner's detect, any other vessel. The spy figured that he's probably early, after all the rendezvous point is practically in the center of an asteroid field.

Several minutes after arriving, a loud beeping sound goes off from the navigational console, and as much to his surprise scanners detect a Chabalarion vessel. He assumed that the contact would be another Drakkorlam, but apparently he was wrong. The spy has never met a Chabalarion before, now that he thinks about it, probably only a handful of Drakkorlam has ever seen one first hand.

"Draqkorlamaque vessel, this is Layroshk of Chabalar. Please land your ship on the largest asteroid to your portside."

"Understood." Responded the Drakkorlam spy.

The scout-ship wasn't equipped with a visual communicator, only audio, therefore both navigators were for the moment unable to see each other. The spy, as he laid in a course for the asteroid, couldn't help but wonder what this Chabalarion or any other one looked like. He had heard rumors describing they looked like, but none were ever confirmed. As he deployed his landing struts, he began to imagine what their appearance would be like. Did they have longer limbs? Were their heads bigger or smaller? Did they look like Draqkor's? Or was it something minor, such as one more, or less, finger than a Drakkorlam?

These of course were all based on rumors that he had heard, and was said on his planet.

Now, in less than a few minutes, he would be one of the few Drakkorlam's to ever make physical contact with a being from Chabalar. Watching the Chabalarion vessel land beside his, he wondered if at least one of the rumors were true, did they really have long tentacles coming out from their side?

"Commander Katrelk." Said Razaal, "I am detecting another vessel."

"I know, long-range scanners indicate it is Chabalarion.”

"Should we now attack?” Asked an eager Razaal.

"Negative. Let them make contact first.”

From beyond detection of the Chabalar and the stolen Draqkorlamaque vessels, they observe from a safe distance as the two ship's make contact with each other.

"Commander, the vessels have established a communications link.” Razaal said, feeling the need to remind his commander, "We can now attack, as ordered.”

"No. Not yet.” Commander Katrelk ordered, "Not until they make physical contact.”

As they got closer, they watched the Draqkorlamaque scout-ship land, followed by the Chabalarion ship.

"Concentrate your firepower on the aft section of the vessels, disabling their engines and therefore preventing them from taking off, after which we will destroy them.”

"As you command.”

"Attack now!!!” Shouted Katrelk.

The Chabalarion vessel lands less then ten meters away from the scout-ship, simultaneously both of the ships' steel hull extended outward, as if reaching for one another. The steel hull almost liquefied itself on one side of each ship, then formed several tendrils. When the metallic tendrils from one ship touched each other, they, meaning the ships, unified. Once unified, the passengers from one vessel can go to the other. The Drakkorlam spy met the Chabalarion halfway the newly formed section of the now unified ship.

"Greetings. I am Layroshk."

"I am Queil, Drakkorlam spy." He said.

Although the Chabalarion didn't notice, the Drakkor-lam spy was a little disappointed. All the rumors he had heard, regarding the appearance of the

Chabalarions, were false and greatly exaggerated. The people of Chabalar, physically, weren't that much different than the people of Drakkorlam. The two species had only one minor difference, they had no nose, at least not where one should be. The Chabalarions breathed through two nostrils, located just below their earlobes.

As the two were about to greet each other physically, they feel the ground shake violently. They both quickly realize that they are being attacked, each runs back to their side of the ship.

"There is no time to detach out vessels!!!" Shouted Queil over the comm-system.

"Then what would you suggest we do?" Layroshk asked.

"I suggest that we work together, literally." Queil said, "You operate the energy blasters, while I navigate the vessel."

"What about the data you have stored in your mind?"

"Get them off our back's first, then worry about the data."

The unified vessel took off and headed deeper into the asteroid field, but that did not stop the Draqkorlamaque ships from following. The unified ship dodged and weaved, turned left and right, went up and under, as many asteroids as possible while at the same time trying to avoid from being fired upon by the two pursuing ships. The asteroids that were impossible to avoid were shot at, however the Draqkorlamaque vessel's did not bother to try and avoid certain asteroids, they simply blasted anything that got in their way.

"Do not lose sight of them." Commander Katrelk said, as his blasted an asteroid three times the size of his ship.

"As you command, sir."

"We must hurry and find shelter before the Draqkor-lamaque ships blast us out of the stars." Queil said.

"On my way to meet you I saw an asteroid with a cavern or cave of some kind." Replied Layroshk, "Perhaps we can temporarily hide inside."

"Surely their scanners would detect us."

"I am not certain. But what other choice do we have?"

"I agree." He said, as one of the computer consoles near the navigational controls short circuit and burst into flames, "So where is it?"

"It was around here somewhere." Said Layroshk looking at every asteroid that they flew by, "There it goes, off the port-bow."

"I see it." Said Queil, "Hang on!" They maneuvered their vessel cautiously into the hollow, cavern-like, asteroid before being discovered.

"The only thing we have to worry about, is keeping this vessel steady while inside" Said Layroshk.

"Why is that?"

"If we do not keep steady, then we will be smashed against the cavern walls of the asteroid."

Keeping the ship steady inside the asteroid proved to be very difficult, due to the artificial gravitational pull. The artificial gravity, even though it was unstable, was created by the asteroid's unpredictable rotation.

The Draqkorlamaque's, after losing them, began to patrol the asteroid field. "Commander." Razaal said, "The scanners are not detecting them anywhere."

"So I have noticed." The Commander replied in annoyance.

"What should we do now?"

"Blast as many asteroids as possible." He ordered, "That should flush them out into the open."

Layroshk and Queil, while preventing themselves from being smashed, could hear the other asteroids being blasted and with each blast getting closer, "We must figure a way to escape without being pursued." Layroshk said.

"There is only one way that I know of, and that is to fight our way out." Said Queil.

"You are correct, however it would be simpler if we could disconnect our ships during mid-flight."

"Look ahead, just below the boulder-like rock, there is a small flat surface of stone where we can land and separate our ships."

As soon as they landed, they began the procedures to disconnect the unified vessels. Again the steel hull from both ships liquefied themselves, this time it detracted instead of extending itself.

"Commander Katrelk." Said Razaal, "There appears to be an opening on the asteroid off the portside of our current position, do you think it is possible that they may have discovered it and gone inside to escape detection."

"Anything is possible." Responded Katrelk, "Let us enter with caution."

They entered the cavern-like asteroid at less the half the speed they were traveling, so as not to fly pass the enemy vessel and to avoid from being smashed against the wall. A few minutes into the asteroid and they locate the ship that they were searching for. Katrelk, who spots it first, yells out, "Open fire!"

The two Draqkor navigators had not noticed that their enemy were in the process of separating the unified vessel. As the blasts from the ships continued, non-stop for a couple of seconds, dust from the asteroids ground lifted, giving cover to the now disconnected ships.

"Now is our chance, before the dust settles!" Shouted Queil through the comm-system, "You engage the lead ship, I'll take care of the other!"

As the dust settled, the Draqkor's assumed that they had accomplished their mission by destroying the enemy. But upon closer observation, they could find no trace of steel wreckage.

"Where did they go?" Asked Katrelk in a low almost whisper, surprised that their blasts had missed their target.

"Commander! Behind us!" Razaal shouted, but it was too late, they had no time to react. Before they knew it, both the Drakkorlam spy and Chabalarion opened fire and destroyed them.

"Now, where were we? Ah, yes. The data." Layroshk said.

After realizing that there was nowhere to land their ship's inside the asteroid, they decide to land outside on the surface of another asteroid. With the two ships once again unified, both navigators are on the scout ship section. Queil is seated on the pilots chair, while Layroshk stood behind him holding a visor-like object.

"Please remain calm after I place this over your eyes." He said, "It will retrieve the data you have gathered."

Layroshk put the visor on Queil, it was pitch dark, he could not see anything. Suddenly, for a few seconds, flashes of different colored lights rushed towards him. Then, just as suddenly, it once again became dark and the visor was removed.

"That is it, we are done." Said Layroshk.

"What about the microchip?" Queil asked.

"Did they not inform you?"

"Inform me of what?"

"Once the data is retrieved from your brain, it will dissolve itself into your bloodstream. As soon as it has dissolved, the host will have no recollection of the data he or she once carried."

"How long does that take?"

"It should be done already. Can you recall any details from the data?"

"No. It would seem that you are correct, although I can still remember the mission, I cannot recall the specifics."

"Then our mission is complete."

Within a few minutes, both ships were disconnected and heading in two different directions, opposite each other. One was heading towards the planet Drakkorlam, and the other towards Chabalar. Even though they were heading opposite ways, they were still able to communicate with each other for awhile.

"Do you think your people will assist us in defending Earth?" Asked Queil.

"If my people feel that Earth is worth defending, then yes, most likely we will assist."

"Farewell my friend, keep safe on your journey home." Queil said.

"Goodbye, and hope you do as well." Responded Layroshk.

CHAPTER – 15

Two days later.

Jason has just arrived at his house from the cemetery. He's alone, sitting on the steps of his back porch toying around with the twenty dollar bill his father had given him. He flipped the bill from one side to the other, remembering what his father had once told him about the silver strip inside. He held it up to the sunlight where he not only noticed the strip, but also a couple of Draqkorlamaque ships flying by. He's been meaning to ask Oubrago about the sudden, almost hostile, change but with his father's death and all, he hasn't had the time.

"Jason!" His mother called for him from inside the house, "Where are you!?!"

"Out here!" He shouted.

His mother comes out to the porch and stands beside him, "You're goin' to leave soon, aren't you?"

"Yeah." He said, looking at his wristwatch, "I have to report back to the Freedom in about three hours."

"Can that fighter of yours carry cargo?" She asked.

"Yeah, why?"

"Come upstairs to the attic with me. There's a few things that belonged to your father, which I'm sure he'd want you to have."

They walked upstairs together and with almost every other step, they would pass by a picture mounted on the wall. They tried not to look at any, but there was one photograph in particular Sandra could not avoid looking at, and that was her wedding picture. The wedding photo was framed on the wall directly in front of the first half of the stairwell before one makes a right to climb the second, and final, half. She stood their for awhile, staring at the picture, specifically at her husband John. He was standing behind her, with his arms wrapped around her waist, wearing his father's black tuxedo. She of course wore a white wedding dress, that was made by her great, great grandmother, which was passed down to the females of her family throughout the generations. She remembers that day so vividly, that she can even recall the sadness she held inside on that day. The sadness had nothing to do with the wedding itself, but with the fact that her mother was not there to see her get married due to her death which was caused by cancer the year before. John knew how she was feeling, so as they posed for the portrait, he whispered in her ear not to worry that her mother was present in spirit.

"Mom, I hate to rush you but--"

"Yes, of course dear. Don't worry." She kissed two of her fingers, then with the same two fingers, touched John's face on the picture before continuing on up the stairs.

Thirty minutes later.

"Mom, I don't think my fighter has enough cargo

space to carry all fifteen boxes."

"Then I guess we'll have to do something so that you can at least take three boxes or so." She said while shifting items from one box to another.

"Mom, wait." Jason said, realizing what she was doing, "I'll tell you what, I'll take these pictures of us, dad, and Aunt Natasha. I'll also take this leather trench jacket he use to like wearing, okay?"

"Fine." She said folding the leather jacket, "It's just that--" Suddenly bursting into tears.

Jason hugs his mother and also begins to tear, not only for the lost of his father, but for his mother. He knows that when he leaves she will be all alone in the house without anybody to talk with, except for his aunt who he knows would come around every so often. Also Oubrago, who would at least spend the night once or twice a week.

Sandra walks Jason to his fighter, watches him put the leather jacket away in the cargo department, located in the rear of the fighter. Jason then kisses his mother goodbye, and climbs aboard. He turns to look at his mother only to see her crying, he climbs back down off his fighter and hugs her tightly for a few seconds.

"Mom… You've gotta stop crying." He tells her, "It makes it hard for me to leave."

"I'll try baby." She said.

Jason again boards his fighter, puts his headgear interface on, while at the same time his mother walked back toward the house. He gave her one final look and, although she kept strong for him by trying not to cry, he could almost see a tear begin to flow down her cheek. She watched the fighter fly into the sky for as long as she could see it, until all that could be seen of the fighter was a small dot, then it disappeared. When she entered the house she locked the door, and sat down on John's favorite chair watching a special report on her H.3-D.T.V. about an incident that had occurred.

"Viewers, what you are about to watch is a video footage taken by a man from Ohio earlier today. We must advise, due to its graphic nature, that children should not watch." Said the reporter.

Sandra could not believe what she was seeing, the video footage showed a commercial airliner getting its wings fired upon by one of the Draqkorlamaque ships, while another ship came from underneath and collided straight through the middle. They repeated the footage twice before the reporter came back on.

"We are now receiving information that other, some worse, incidents are now occurring all over the world." Said the reporter, "We advise that viewers remain in their homes till further news is developed."

"Oh my God!" Said Sandra in disbelief.

Oubrago is standing near the Briggs' front door when she suddenly gets a message, mentally from Duural, "What is it?"

"Is it clear for us to communicate?" Duural asked.

"Yes, go on." Responded Oubrago, mentally, before entering the house.

"We have an urgent situation Oubrago."

"What kind of situation?"

"It appears that the Draqkor's have become aggressive during the past twenty-four hours."

"Please explain." She said.

"The Draqkorlamaque's have destroyed several of the human airplane's."

"How many have they destroyed?"

"Nine have been confirmed."

Oubrago was in shock at what she had just heard, she was in so much shock that she felt the need to sit on the steps of the front porch.

"Oubrago?" Duural asked, "Are you still there?"

She took awhile before answering, but she eventually did, "Yes, I'm here." She responded, looking up at the sky as if though she were able to see Duural's ship. "I can still hear you."

"Then what should we do?"

"Nothing."

"What!?!"

"At least for now." She said, "Remain low, the time for fighting will soon present itself, but for now tell the others to do the same."

"Very well." He complied, "Duural out."

Oubrago stayed sitting outside the house for a little longer, admiring the beauty of this planet. She's thinking about whether she did the right thing by empowering a young human boy with the skills and knowledge, which was given to her people genetically. But her quiet moment was abruptly cut short, as she noticed several Draqkor Enforcers standing in front of a few houses, including Jason's house.

"What is the meaning of this? Who ordered you here!?!" Oubrago demanded to know, as she got up from the porch steps.

"We were ordered by Zard to standby and handle any resistance that may occur when the attack begins." Answered the commanding Enforcer.

Before Oubrago can ask another question, a couple of Enforcers stormed inside a house directly across the Briggs'. A commotion was heard from within the house, it was the sound of furniture being thrown around. Then it became silent, and Oubrago thought of the worst. Shortly after the silence, the Enforcers that entered the house came from the backyard carrying two young boys. The two boys looked so much alike that anyone would think they were twins, they ranged between eight and twelve years of age. Even though the boys were being carried out, they still put up a struggle, as well did their parents, who were being dragged against their will by the neck. A crowd begins to form, which the Draqkorlamaque's are keeping in control. People are everywhere, trying to get a better view, some are standing in front of their house doors, and others are scattered around the block.

"Commander." Said one of the Enforcers to the one talking with Oubrago, "These two were throwing objects at my Enforcers. What should we do with them?"

The Draqkorlamaque Commander looked at the two

boys and their parents, then looked at the crowd of humans that has gathered around them, "I think we should make examples of these two by executing them." He said.

"What about these other two?" The Enforcer asked, pushing the parents to the ground.

"We shall take them to the Avoloxzia, and slaughter them there."

The boys were then separated from their parents, but not without a struggle. Their father fought them with every ounce of strength he had, but he was struck on the back of the head by one of the Enforcers, knocking him unconscious. The crowd began to react by yelling obscenities at them, but they were quickly silenced when one of the Draqkor Enforcers pulled out his energy blaster, aimed at one child's head and fired, killing him instantly.

"No!!!" Screamed Oubrago, but it was too late. The bodies dropped hard to the ground and their blood splattered on several people's clothing as well as on their parents clothing.

"Take these two humans, as well as this sympathizer, to the Avoloxzia." Ordered the Commanding Enforcer, "As for the crowd, disperse them. If they resist, execute them."

Four Draqkor Enforcers escorted Oubrago and the two humans to a scout ship, located five blocks away from the Briggs' house. The scout ship doors opened and formed steps, and the two humans were taken inside followed by Oubrago. All three were seated in a row next to each other with one Enforcer between the two humans and the other between Oubrago and the female. The other two Enforcers sat behind the navigational console and prepared for take-off. The human female was crying uncontrollably over the death of her children, while her husband was in so much shock that he had an almost blank stare in his eyes.

"Stop your crying human!" Shouted the Enforcer seated between her and Oubrago. But she did not stop crying, instead she cried even louder. The Enforcer then got up from the seat and stood in front of her.

"I said stop your crying human!" The Enforcer said again, in anger, "I will not repeat myself again!"

"That is correct, you will not have the opportunity of repeating yourself because I am going to kill you." Said Oubrago, who caused a distraction by revealing her true identity. She then made a fist and pointed her arm directly at the Enforcer seated between her and the human female, firing an energy blast into his head, then she fired again at the Enforcer seated next to the male. Oubrago quickly grabbed the energy weapon from the first Draqkor Enforcers body and tossed it over toward the human male.

"I suggest you learn how to use one of those within the next three seconds." Oubrago said.

One of the Draqkor's that was sitting on the navigational chair quickly got up and fired at Oubrago, nearly hitting her on the shoulder. The human male aimed the energy weapon at the navigator and fired, hitting the Draqkor on the chest. The other navigator didn't have a chance, Oubrago ran up to him and blasted him on the back of the neck.

"Come on." Said Oubrago, "Let us get out of here."

"Where will we go?" The human female asked.

"Yeah, won't they be looking for us?" Asked the human male.

"Not unless I take you somewhere safe." Oubrago answered, "And I know just the place. Hang on, and please remain seated."

CHAPTER – 16

"I don't get it." A puzzled Jason said, "The U.S.S. Freedom should be here. This is the rendezvous point, isn't it?"

"YES IT IS." Replied Chrisash.

"Any sign of them on the scanners?"

"NO."

"Have you noticed that there aren't as many Draqkorlamaque ships in the vicinity as when we left for Earth."

"YES. PERHAPS THAT IS THE REASON WHY THE U.S.S. FREEDOM IS NOT HERE."

"Or, perhaps, it's exactly why the U.S.S. Freedom isn't here."

"PLEASE EXPLAIN YOURSELF JASON."

"It's simple. Maybe the U.S.S. Freedom got overwhelmed, maybe even attacked by the Draqkorlamaque vessel's. Who knows, probably the U.S.S. Freedom was destroyed."

"WE WOULD KNOW." Chrisash said.

"What?"

"WE WOULD KNOW." The ship repeated.

"How?"

"IF THE U.S.S. FREEDOM WAS DESTROYED, THERE WOULD HAVE BEEN METAL DEBRIS IN THIS REGION OF SPACE." The ship explained.

"Yeah, okay. Maybe you're right."

"SCANNERS ARE DETECTING A SHIP DIRECTLY AHEAD."

"What kind of ship?"

"A DRAQKORLAMAQUE SHIP. SHOULD I ENGAGE EVASIVE MANEUVERS?"

"No, not yet. Let's see what they want first?"

"SHOULD I TARGET THE SHIP?"

"Negative."

The Draqkorlamaque ship swooped past Jason at such a close range that he would swear, if it were possible, that he could touch it's steel hull. Jason quickly turned his fighter hard about, but it wasn't fast enough, the alien ship had already stopped and had a target lock on his fighter. Chrisah automatically activated its targeting system, however, it didn't have time to open fire because just as the ship switched on its systems, the Draqkorlamaque ship exploded.

"What were you waiting for to open fire?" Said a voice over the comm-system, "An invitation?"

"Ha–ha, very funny Jiggy." Jason sarcastically answered, quickly guessing who it was that was talking to him, "Where's the U.S.S. Freedom?"

"Follow me Jason, it's not safe to be out here for a long period of time." Jason followed Jesus to the planet Pluto where the U.S.S. Freedom, along with three other ships similar in design and size to that of the Freedom, were in a low standard orbit behind one another.

"What's going on Jiggy?" Jason asked, "Where did

those other three spacecraft carrier's come from and what are they doing here?"

"Well Jason, it's obvious that they came from Earth. But as for the reason why they're here, is for protection."

"What do you mean by protection?"

"While you were on Earth, the Freedom received reports that the Draqkors were acting hostile. Did you notice anything weird about them while you were their?"

"Yeah." Said Jason.

"Like what?"

"Like what assumed to be Draqkor soldiers patrolling the streets, and ships following me around. It was as if though they knew who belonged on Earth and who didn't."

"Was that all?" Jiggy asked.

"Yeah. What else was suppose to happen?"

"Well for starters, Draqkorlamaque ships have been reported to be colliding into commercial airliners. And those soldiers you mentioned, they're doing more than patrolling, they were killing people."

"I didn't see any of that while I was down there." Said Jason.

"This is Jesus Rodriguez to the U.S.S. Freedom, requesting clearance to dock." He said as they approached the starboard side of the spacecraft carrier.

"Affirmative." Said an officer through the comm-system from the U.S.S. Freedom, "Remain on course and prepare for docking procedures."

"Roger that Freedom." Replied Jiggy.

"This is Jason Briggs, also requesting clearance to dock."

"Negative. Please standby for further orders, U.S.S. Freedom out."

"Well Jiggy, I guess I'll be seeing you later." Jason watched as his friends' ship docked in the Freedom. Even though Oubrago had told and showed him certain things, he still tried to make sense as to why the Draqkorlamaque's would kill human people. However, he didn't have much time to figure out the current situation, due to the voice on the comm-system.

 "U.S.S. Freedom to Jason Briggs, please respond."

"Go ahead, Freedom." Jason answered.

"Your orders are to report to the U.S.S. Sedgwick and escort Captain Lindquist here."

"Understood." He said, "Changing course and heading towards the U.S.S. Sedgwick."

Jason has never been inside another spacecraft carrier, other than the U.S.S. Freedom. He wondered, as he flew past both the U.S.S. Reagan and the U.S.S. Roddenberry, whether the interior of all these spacecraft carrier's were identical to the U.S.S. Freedom as they appeared to be on the exterior. As he approached the Sedgwick, he began to think about his mother. He wondered if she was in any danger, he also hoped that the reports were mistaken, that the Draqkor were not doing what was being reported.

"U.S.S. Sedgwick, this is Jason Briggs from the U.S.S. Freedom, requesting permission to dock."

CHAPTER – 16

"Permission granted." Said a female voice, "proceed to the main docking-bay."

As he landed his fighter and began to take off his headgear, he noticed that there were three other fighter pilots standing near their fighters. He hopped off his fighter and also stood near it, looking around and noticing that the docking-bay was identical to that of the U.S.S. Freedom. That answered his question, the entire ship, including the other two, must be the same as his. He also noticed another ship, this one was much bigger than a fighter even though the design was similar to a fighter.

"All visiting escort fighter pilots, please board your fighters and prepare for launch." Said the same female voice from before through the comm-system.

Jason boarded his fighter and after a few minutes he saw four figures enter the docking-bay, though he couldn't make out any details because they entered through a door on the far side. He knew one was a female and assumed that was Captain Lindquist, due to the way she was being escorted toward the larger fighter. Moments after they boarded, the engines started.

"This is Captain Lindquist onboard the U.S.S. Sedgwick command shuttle, all escort fighters please depart from the carrier and assume standard escort formation."

All fighters took off from the spacecraft carrier, at minimum speed, and presumed escort positions. A few seconds later, the command shuttle took its position. A standard escort formation calls for the command shuttle to take its position in the center, between four fighters. The positions of the four fighters would be one fighter above and below, while the other two were in front and behind the shuttle. As Jason flew by the other spacecraft carriers, he noticed other command shuttles being escorted toward the U.S.S. Freedom.

"Chrisash?"

"YES JASON." The ship answered.

"Why do you suppose all these command shuttle's are going to the U.S.S. Freedom?"

"I AM NOT CERTAIN JASON. PERHAPS IT HAS SOMETHING TO DO WITH THE REPORTS I HAVE BEEN RECEIVING FROM EARTH."

"What kind of reports?"

"IT APPEARS THAT THE DRAQKOR'S HAVE BEEN DESTROYING AIRLINERS AND HAVE ALSO SEIZED COMMAND OF CERTAIN CITIES AND STATES, AS WELL AS COUNTRIES."

"What about New York, specifically the Bronx?"

"NOTHING HAS BEEN REPORTED ABOUT THE EAST COAST. HOWEVER THE ENTIRE WEST COAST OF NORTH AMERICA IS UNDER DRAQKOR RULE."

"What do you mean nothing? There has to be something?"

Chrisash remained silent for a couple of seconds.

"Well?" Jason asked.

"SCANNING FOR MEDIA REPORTS OF THE EAST COAST." Again, the ship remained silent.

CHAPTER – 16

"Found anything yet?"

"YES. THE PRESIDENT HAS BEEN MOVED TO AN UNDISCLOSED LOCATION AND SOME CITIES ARE FIGHTING BACK – –"

"What about the Bronx, are they fighting back?"

"YES. BUT NOT ALL THE BOROUGHS. STATEN ISLAND AND QUEENS ARE UNDER DRAQKOR RULE."

It was Jason who now remained silent, as he looked in the direction of Earth. Although he could not see the planet, due to the distance, he thought about his mother's safety and that of the thousands of people being killed worldwide.

"Attention all command shuttles and escorts, this is the U.S.S. Freedom, requesting that you please maintain your positions till further notice. Freedom out."

Within minutes, all of the command shuttles and escorts were docking in the U.S.S. Freedom. Upon landing, the three visiting Captain's were greeted by Capt. Wilkins and were each being escorted by one the fighter pilots from their spacecraft carriers, to the war room.

CHAPTER – 17

The location of the war room is near the bridge of the U.S.S. Freedom. It has two entrances, one from the bridge, and the other from the main corridor leading to the bridge. The war room's location is identical in all spacecraft carriers, however, the interior decorations of the room is entirely up to the captain of the individual ship.

The U.S.S. Freedom's war room has an authentic, wooden feel to it. Captain Wilkins made certain that it be made from Red Oak, which he considered to be one of the strongest and finest wood. The floor is made of wooden boards to match the varnished, wooden paneled walls. The oval conference table, and chairs, are also made of wood. On the table itself there are operational flat screen computers already opened for viewing. To one side of the room there are two large view ports to observe the wondrous void of space, also on the same side of the view ports, to the right, are a couple of computer consoles. On the other side to the left, is a complementary bar built just for pleasure, complete with all kinds of alcoholic and non-alcoholic beverages.

"Fellow Captains." Said Capt. Wilkins, who sat on one side of the table, "As you are well aware by now, relations between alien and humans have changed for the worse."

Seated to the right of Captain Wilkins was the captain of the U.S.S. Roddenberry, Capt. Antonio De La Rosa. He is the youngest of the four captains, with long, shoulder length, jet black hair. Seated across from him was a tall slender woman, with short blonde hair, who's name was Rachel Lindquist, Captain of the U.S.S. Sedgwick. To the right of her was the captain of the U.S.S. Reagan, Capt. James Linwood. Captain Linwood has long, brown, braided hair that reached halfway down his back. Everyone knew he worked out physically, due to the muscular arms and broad shoulders.

"Yes, we've read the transmitted reports coming from Earth." Said Capt. Lindquist.

"Then you also know that the President should be in route to a secured location." Capt. Wilkins said as he signaled for wine to be served, "And as a result of that we were summoned here to listen and follow his orders recorded prior to his relocation." He paused to take a sip of wine, "If there aren't any questions, then let us proceed."

The four captains pressed the play button on the table desktop computers, and immediately on the screen appeared a digitally enhanced picture of Earth, rotating. The screen then split in two, placing the picture of Earth on one side and the recording of President Williams on the other.

"Captains of the four spacecraft carriers." Said the President, looking a little nervous, "By now you are aware that the Draqkor's have begun their invasion of Earth. I have very little time so I will make this short, seeing as how this is being recorded during transit to a top secret government installation. I am asking for a simple request, take back Earth and protect its people. I will leave you now, with the confidence in knowing that the four of you, under Capt. Wilkin's command, will carry out my request. May whatever God you believe in, if any, protect you and the entire human race. Good luck." The President, who was seated behind a desk during this little speech, stood and gave a salute before the picture of Earth reverted to its original full screen size.

Capt. Wilkins closed the flat top computer, stood up from his seat, while at the same time grabbing his glass of wine. He took a sip as he walked toward the bar, where he then placed the glass down. Then he walked to one of the view ports, crossed his arms and stared out into space. As he began to think of a plan, the other three captains closed their computers. The crewmate, who was assigned to serve as bartender, began to go around the table and offered more wine. But all three captains turned down the offer, and instead waited patiently for Capt. Wilkins to try and devise a plan.

He inhaled then exhaled deeply, soaking in the new responsibility that has been thrust upon his shoulders. Capt. Wilkins knows that any command he makes will have casualties and consequences, which he would have very little, or no control over. He walked back to the table to rejoin the other captains, he sat back down and looked at all three of them, noticing how much younger than him they were. But he knew, through thick and thin, they would follow his orders.

"Return to your respected spacecraft carriers." Capt. Wilkins said, "In seventy-two hours, we will attack their mother-ship, and defend Earth."

"How? With what plan?" Asked Capt. Linwood.

"I will transmit the plans for operation 'Take Back Earth' in forty-eight hours." Assured Capt. Wilkins, "For the moment, place your ships on high alert… If anyone has any questions now's the time to ask them, if not, you are all dismissed." As Captains Lindquist, Linwood, and De La Rosa walked out the war room, Capt. Wilkins stayed and began to devise a strategic and precise plan...

There are three Draqkorlamaque Enforcers standing guard in front of every house and apartment building of every borough in New York, they have made it clear that a curfew has been put into effect. That if anybody came out of their homes, they would taken to the mother-ship and await execution. Reports of the curfew issued, unofficially, by the Draqkor have reached the entire world in a matter of hours, and just as quickly the Enforcer's were dispatched. Some cities and countries fought the curfew, but from the beginning the Enforcer's proved to be much more superior. The latest report witnessed by the world was of a reporter being executed by a Draqkor Enforcer, live on national television, for breaking curfew.

Maggie, who was one of the billions of viewers, watched as the reporters body dropped to the cement ground. She was so disgusted that she speed walked to her window, where she not only saw the Enforcers standing in front of hers and other people's houses, but she also witnessed them entering some of the home's and take people against their will.

Maggie felt outraged and wanted to do something about the situation, but her brother beat her to it. She watched from the living room window as Jacob, with a wooden baseball bat in his hand, came out of the house ready to swing at one of the Enforcers.

Jacob swung the bat furiously at one of the Enforcers head, she knew he must have killed the Draqkor instantly when she saw that the alien's head split open like a watermelon upon impact. The other Enforcer standing guard next to the now dead one, immediately apprehended Jacob. Maggie and her parents quickly run outside, screaming and yelling hysterically, to get Jacob from the Draqkor Enforcer.

Enforcer's, who were standing guard outside other nearby houses, rushed over and grabbed Maggie and her parents, throwing them all face down on the ground. They were held there, against their will, while Jacob was being dragged away kicking and screaming.

"Where are you takin'g him!?!" Jacob's father demanded to know, as he tried to get up.

"That should be of no concern to you." Answered one of the Enforcers.

"As his father, I have a right to know!" He said, as he again tried to get up from the ground.

"He will be transported to the Avoloxzia, where he will be executed for killing an Enforcer."

"Please forgive my son. He's young, he doesn't know any better. You should take me instead." Pleaded their father.

"You are correct, he is young, perhaps he did not

know better." Said an Enforcer, assisting Jacob's father up from the ground and wiping some of the dirt from his clothing.

"Then, you're going to let him go?"

"No. We are taking you as well." The Enforcer said as he pushed him toward another Enforcer, who then proceeded to take him in the same direction as his son.

"No!" Screamed Maggie's mother, as she watched them take both her husband and son away.

An Enforcer suddenly grabbed her by the hair and pulled her up from the ground, "Shut your mouth human!" He shouted.

Maggie could not see what the Enforcer was doing to her mother, all she could see was her mother's feet dangling in mid-air frantically kicking at the alien. Suddenly her mother's feet stopped kicking and didn't move at all, neither did she hear her yelling anymore. She did however, see blood poor down her mother's feet, quickly forming a puddle. Maggie wanted to scream, but thought that if she did she would probably end up like her mother, whose body was tossed a few feet away. She didn't realize it at first, that although her mother's body landed face down, her head which was crushed like a grape, was facing upward.

"What shall we do with this one?" Asked the Enforcer who had her pinned on the ground with his foot.

"I suggest we do the same with her as we did to her mother." Said another Enforcer.

Upon agreement by the Enforcers, Maggie was hoisted up from the ground much in the same way as her mother was. She knew that she was going to end up like her mother unless she did something. The Enforcer held her body up by the neck with one hand, and began to palm her face with the other, instinctively she bit off one of the aliens long fingers. The Enforcer dropped her, as he yelled and clenched his hand in pain. Maggie of course didn't hesitate, she ran as fast as she could toward Jason's house wiping the purple liquid from her face and mouth, which she assumed to be the Enforcers blood.

CHAPTER – 18

Sandra is alone in the house, unaware of what has happened across the street. She's looking out the window noticing that the lawn on her backyard appeared to be a little dry, almost yellow in color. She then began thinking of how much John enjoyed watering the yard, but hated mowing the lawn. Her thinking, however, is abruptly interrupted by a strong, sudden, wind blowing at the window. At first she was excited, she thought it was Jason's ship, that he had returned home. But she realized that the size and shape was different. It was a Draqkorlamaque ship, like the one they used for a school trip about six years ago, which had just touched down on her backyard.

"What the Hell?" She said, as three figure emerged from the ship.

Recognizing two of the three figures were her next door neighbors, she ran outside to assist whoever or whatever it was that's helping them. All the years Sandra lived next door to them, which was about seven years, she never knew their names. Not many people in the neighborhood did, they never bothered anybody, they always kept to themselves.

"What happened?" Sandra asked, seeing the look of shock on her neighbors faces.

"It is a long story, Sandra." Answered Oubrago, as she assisted the human female across the lawn.

"Who are you and how do you know my name?" Sandra asked while assisting her other neighbor by the arm.

"It is I, Oubrago."

"That's impossible, the Oubrago that I know doesn't look like that, her skin isn't orange."

"Actually, it is." Said Oubrago, as they entered the house, "I suggest you have a seat while I explain what has happened and, why I disguised myself."

After an hour of proving she was Oubrago, which she accomplished by telling Sandra about the first encounter between herself and Jason, she began tinkering with the device on her waist belt. The device was small, nearly unnoticeable, it was attached to her belt buckle which held her side arm gun. She wore a leather brown, vest-like, trench jacket with what looked like gray spandex pants and brown leather boots.

Sandra watched as the alien, who claimed to be Oubrago, tried to repair the device, "What does that thing do?" She asked.

"This device, which I assume was damaged during our escape, enables me to disguise myself holographically." Said Oubrago, feeling frustrated that she couldn't get it to work.

"Can I see it?"

Oubrago disconnected the device from her belt buckle, and handed it to Sandra. The device was as thin as a credit card and weighed just as light, which was surprising to her considering it was made of some kind of steel alloy. She looked at it for a while, as she examined it, she noticed that one side had a smooth surface. But the other side had two tiny, square-like, holes on opposite ends with markings carved between them. Sandra took a hairpin from her hair and put it through one of the holes, moved it around, expecting something to happen, but nothing did. She then did the same thing to the other hole, but again nothing happened. She took a closer look at the device, then glanced over at Oubrago, and without a warning she banged it against the wall twice, causing the two holes on the devise to light up.

"I think that did it." Said Sandra, handing the device back to Oubrago.

Oubrago then placed it back on her buckle, and the alien Sandra once knew and has grown to trust, again appeared. "I do not know how you did it, Sandra, but I thank you for repairing the holographic device." Oubrago said.

"Oubrago." Said Sandra, "It really is you."

"Were you still in doubt?"

Sandra didn't answer her, due to someone knocking on her front door, "Wait a minute, please." She said as Oubrago and the two neighbors hurried up the stairs, toward the attic, to hide.

"Who is it?" She said, cautiously approaching the door to look through the peephole.

"It's me, Maggie." She answered, sounding fatigued.

Sandra quickly opens the door, and just as quickly had to grab Maggie to prevent her from falling, "Oh, God." She uttered, as Maggie collapsed in her arms.

"And this is your plan?" Said Capt. Lindquist, of the U.S.S. Sedgwick.

The four Captains were in their own respected spacecraft carriers, communicating from their table top computers. On the top left corner of the screens were small images of the other three captains, with a 3-D image of the tactical plan proposed by Capt. Wilkins.

"Yes, and I know it will work." Capt. Wilkins assured them, "Just hear me out."

Captain Wilkins made certain that the computers image of the plan repeated itself to coincide with his explanation, which showed all four spacecraft carriers. Two going toward, then orbiting, an image of Earth, while the other two went toward an image of the Avoloxzia. "The U.S.S. Roddenberry and the U.S.S. Reagan will go to Earth, one will orbit vertically from North to South and the other from horizontally from East to West. After which, they will deploy all space fighters to prevent other Draqkorlamaque ships from entering or leaving Earth. The U.S.S. Sedgwick and my ship, the Freedom, will travel to their mother-ship and hopefully destroy it."

"How are you going to destroy the mother-ship?" Capt. De La Rosa asked, "Do you have a plan for that?"

"No… Not yet."

"This isn't a plan, it's suicide." Said Capt. Linwood, "Please tell me you're not going to follow through with this, it's crazy."

"Yes I am, and so are all of you, no matter how crazy it sounds." Capt. Wilkins said.

A female crewmember leans over and whispers something to Capt. Wilkins, "Are you certain?" He asked her.

"Yes sir." She replied. Like a domino effect, the other three captains were notified by either a crewmember or first officer of the tragic news.

"By now all of you have been notified that the President's plane, Air Force One, has been shot down somewhere over Nevada. As of this moment, as so ordered by the President, I am hereby assuming full responsibility of Earth's safety. Due to the current situation, operation 'Take Back Earth' will commence in twenty-four hours. Therefore, I order all ships to prepare for battle."

Capt. Wilkins then shuts his computer off, gets down on his knees and begins to pray, "In the name of the father, the son, and the holy spirit…"

Maggie is lying unconscious on the living room couch of the Briggs' house, where Sandra is wiping her face with a cold wet cloth. She suddenly begins to mumble something, although Sandra and Oubrago don't understand what she is saying.

"She appears to be coming out of it." Said Oubrago, as she kneeled beside her.

"Yes, thank God." Sandra said while changing cloth's.

"Mom!!!" Yells Maggie, as she suddenly wakes up, hysterically crying.

Oubrago and Sandra were both startled by the way she suddenly came out of her, somewhat, sleep.

"It's okay dear." Sandra said, hugging her and rocking back and forth with her, "You're safe now."

"Yes, no harm will come to you here." Oubrago reassured her.

Maggie, very violently, pushes Oubrago to the floor, stand over her with a clenched fist ready to strike her, "Stay away from me!"

"Stop it Maggie!" Yelled Sandra, as she grabbed her hand.

"It was her people who killed my mother and took both my father and brother!"

"What, wait. There's a misunderstanding here." Sandra said, "Please, sit down and relax." Pointing at the couch.

Maggie sat back down on the couch she was laying on, while Sandra helped Oubrago up from the floor.

"Since we're all seated now, Maggie, please explain what happened to you."

"It's exactly as I said. Her people, the Draqkorlamaque's murdered my mother, and took my father and brother to their mother-ship."

"I am certain my people did no such thing." Said Oubrago.

"She's telling the truth, Maggie."

"But I saw them Sandra, I saw them with my own two eyes."

"Show her." Sandra told Oubrago.

"Show me what?"

Oubrago remained quiet for a while, then got up from where she was sitting and touched the device on her belt buckle, revealing her true identity to be seen, "I am not a Draqkor."

"What the Hell, who, what are you?"

"I am a Half-breed."

"A what?"

"A Half-breed. My species were genetically engineered to be slaves for the Draqkor, but we fought for our freedom."

"Hold up, you're telling me that your people are Draqkor clone's. that's impossible."

"Why would you say that?"

"Well for starters, your skin complexion is orange, not to mention, you look almost human. The only thing you have in common with them is the fact that you have no hair."

"We were genetically cloned from a combination of Draqkor and Chabalarion D.N.A."

"Chaba-what?" Asked Maggie.

"Chabalarion"

"Who are they?"

"They are inhabitants from the planet Chabalar." Said Oubrago, "Chabalar is much like your Earth. It has had its discoveries and its wars, all on a global scale. However, what it has now is much greater than any of its discoveries, and that is peace. The people of Chabalar have been in peace for well over twelve centuries, they have had no cause for war against anything or anyone, not since the invasion of the planet Korlak."

"Who invaded Korlak, and why?" Maggie curiously asked.

"The Draqkor, as you now know, are very deceitful. They make contact under the guise of peace, when in fact their true intentions is to 'Colonize' the planet, and take the technology it may have."

"But why Earth?" Maggie wanted to know, "What could we have that they would want? I mean correct me if I'm wrong, but aren't they much more advanced than we are?"

"Yes. But they are not here to take your technology, they are here to punish you."

"Punish us for what?" Asked Sandra.

"For stealing their technology."

"What? That's crazy. How did we steal their technology?" Asked Sandra in disbelief.

"During the Earth year of 1947. two unidentified flying objects crash landed near a small town called Roswell. One of the ships had prisoners in it, my people, the other was full of Draqkorlamaque Enforcers. Both of them were small patrol ships, which can hold approximately four to six individuals."

"I don't get it, what does that have to do with anything?" Maggie asked, as she got up from the couch and walked toward the window facing the backyard where she noticed the Draqkorlamaque shuttle.

"The Draqkor believe that the people of Earth have

advanced, very rapidly, as a result of the incident."

"But who's to say we wouldn't have advanced on our own, I mean, if in fact we did steal their technology." Maggie said.

"My people and I agree, but the Draqkorlamaques, however, disagree. They believe that the human species would still be at least two hundred years less technologically advanced than they are today."

"So what are they planning to do about it?" Asked Sandra.

"They are planning to do the same as they did to some of the other planets in my solar system."

"And what's that?" Asked Sandra's neighbor, Charles, which everyone thought was still in the next room.

"They will 'Colonize' your planet."

A silence came over the living room, they all just stared at each other. Maggie then stared out the window, again, looking at the shuttle.

"Can you stop them?" Sandra asked.

"It is not that simple."

"Why not?" Asked Maggie in doubt, "Don't you have more of those holographic thingies?"

"No. However, there are other Half-breeds on board the mother-ship, disguising themselves like I did."

"Well, can't you and your people do something?" Charles asked.

"No… You must understand, there are only a hand-ful of my kind on board, there really is not much we can do."

"Yes there is." Said Maggie, still looking out the window with a devilish grin on her face, "You can pretend that we're your prisoners and pilot that shuttle right into the mother-ship."

"But what will that accomplish?" Asked Oubrago.

"The element of surprise, that's what."

CHAPTER – 19

Chabalar, the inhabitants of this planet have secluded themselves from the rest of the solar system. Not since they tried to defend the planet Korlak has anyone heard from them or about them, not until several weeks ago, when two spies, one from Chabalar and the other from the planet Drakkorlam, met in secret. The meeting was in regards to a Draqkor situation on the rise, and as a result of the information retrieved from the spies, a combined armada consisting of both species from the planets have assembled and are orbiting the moon of Chabalar. The moon is named Kron, it has four massive continents scattered throughout the two bodies of water, or oceans, and the climate is always moderately warm. There are also several rivers, lakes and ponds on each of the continents, as well as forests. Two of the continents are uninhabited, but the other two are used for manufacturing space vessels and armaments. All of the vessels are conceived on the moon's surface, but are assembled in orbit.

The Chabalarion vessels were all designed similar in shape, but varied in size. The smaller, single pilot, attack cruisers are the quickest the fleet has. The cockpit, which was located in the front narrow part of the oval bulb-like shaped ship, was designed with a gyroscopic compartment that allowed it to complete a three hundred sixty degree spin without the navigator feeling it. The bulb-like shape gave the ship a sleek look, and quick action maneuverability, however, its armament was minimal. It is equipped with one laser cannon located on the bow of the vessel, underneath the cockpit. Mounted on the wings of the propulsion systems were two, low yielding missiles. The larger, two manned, vessels are slower in terms of maneuverability, but is much more heavily armed. It has two laser cannons, one below and above the cockpit, and six missiles, three on each wing.

The Chabalarion's didn't build many mother-ship size vessels, they only had five and two of them were being dispatched to defend Earth. The size of the two mother-ships are equivalent to the Draqkor mother-ship, Avoloxzia, and nearly identical in both size and shape. The reasons for the similarities between the ships was due to the schematics, which were stolen by a Chabalarion spy. The Drakkorlams didn't have the resources to build there own ship, they would just steal them, however, they never were able to steal a mother-ship. They instead were navigating Draqkorlamaque attack cruisers and shuttles that were refitted with armaments. There are well over fifteen thousand ships orbiting Kron, all making last minute preparations for Earth.

"This is Queil, of Drakkorlam, to the Chabalar mother-ships." Said Queil, who was onboard the leading shuttle.

"This is the mother-ship Lork, go on." Responded a female from the leading mother-ship.

"On behalf of my fleet, we are requesting permission

to dock."

"Request granted." A different voice responded, a male's voice, "You all can dock on either the Lork or the Quern."

"Layroshk? Is that you?" Asked Queil.

"Yes, and that's Captain Layroshk." He said, "Are you in command of your people's armada?"

"Yes."

"Then I suggest you dock onboard the Quern where I can brief you, in person, concerning an urgent matter."

Although Queil had read reports about the Chabalarions constructing several

Mother-ships based on Draqkor designs, he had never been inside of one. As he was being escorted to the bridge by two Chabalarion escorts, a male and female, he could not help but think how large this vessel really was. He tried to calculate how much cargo capacity a vessel like this must have, and of how many crew members it can house comfortably. He also tried to figure out how much armament a ship of this size had, but by the time he tried to come up with an answer he was already on the bridge.

"Welcome onboard the Quern." Said Layroshk, greeting him by the entrance door of the bridge.

"Thank you Layroshk." Queil said, looking around at the bridge in amazement.

Layroshk guided Queil to all the different stations of the bridge, explaining the various locations and systems each workstation has control over. "This is all fascinating, but earlier you mentioned something about an urgent matter?"

"Yes I did." Said Layroshk, as he lead Queil to the center of the bridge, "Crewman, upload the data on to the main view screen."

The view screen was mounted in the front, center, of the bridge. It was thinly flat and appeared to be built onto the metallic bulkhead panels of the ship, it was eight feet long and six feet wide. At first there was nothing on the screen, it was completely dark, and for that brief moment all that could be seen were the reflections of the bridge crew. Suddenly an image appeared, it was fuzzy and unfocussed at first, but then it sharpened.

"I do not understand, It is just a ship." Said Queil, looking at Layroshk.

"Please, continue to watch." Layroshk replied.

As the image sharpened, it began to widen its view, revealing more of the Draqkorlamaque vessel. The vessel was identical to that of the Avoloxzia, but it became apparent to Queil that this ship was quite different. The image was of a massive Draqkorlamaque fleet assembling, but it wasn't the amount of vessels that surprised Queil, it was the size of the newly built Draqkorlamaque mother-ship. The Avoloxzia was thought to be the largest ship of its time to be constructed, but when compared to the new vessel, it looked like a small scout ship. Queil remained silent as he watched other Draqko-rlamaque mother-ships, equivalent in size to the Avoloxzia, pass by. He couldn't believe how they dwarfed in size when compared to the menacing, unnamed, mother-ship.

"How are we going to get through them?" Asked Queil. He was so concerned about the size of the enemy vessel, that he didn't turn away from the view screen to look at Layroshk.

"Of that I am not certain… Yet." Layroshk replied.

"There is no plan?" He asked in doubt.

"No. That is why I asked that you dock on my ship, perhaps together we can come up with a solution."

"How long do we have before we engage them in battle?"

"We will be utilizing our F.T.L. propulsions as soon as all ships check in,
after which we will be within firing range of the Draqkorlamaque armada in two hours."

"The armada we can manage," Said Queil, who was standing near Layroshk in
the rear section of the bridge looking at a smaller view screen, staring at the size of the Draqkorlamaque fleet and, at the large unnamed mother-ship. "It is the mother-ship that will give us the problem."

"Do not worry yourself about the mother-ship." Said Layroshk.

"Have you thought of a plan?" Queil asked.

"Yes."

"Then continue."

"Captain, we are approaching battle range." Interrupted a crewmember.

"Very well. All personnel report to battle stations!"

"Wait, what about the plan?"

"Do not concern yourself with the plan. For now just get yourself onboard the Lork."

"I do not understand?" A confused Queil asked. Suddenly the ship shook violently from the impact of firepower which struck the starboard side of the ship, causing everybody onboard to lose there balance and sparks to burst into flame from various workstations.

"Attention all ships!" Said Layroshk, as his voice was being transmitted all throughout the Quern as well as every ship in the armada, "As of this moment, I am hereby placing Queil in command of the Lork and the entire fleet."

"What?" Asked Queil, "What about you?"

"Crewmen, please escort commander Queil to his shuttle." Said Layroshk, pointing at the two guards standing watch by the bridge entrance, "Anyone who feels the urge to leave, may do so. You will not be looked upon any different."

"This is suicide!" Shouted Queil, as the guards began to take him against his will, "I know what you plan on doing!"

Layroshk watched as the guards, forcefully, escorted Queil away. He expected a majority of his bridge officers and crew to follow, but they all remained at their stations as did the entire crew of the ship.

As Queil boarded his shuttle, the Quern shook again, but

not as bad as it did when he was on the bridge. His shuttle, along with three attack cruisers, were the only vessels on the docking-bay that were preparing for launch.

"Navigators, prepare for departure." Ordered Queil, taking his seat directly behind one of the navigators.

"Yes sir." They both acknowledged.

The Quern shook yet again, this time much more violently than the first time, causing bursts of flames and explosions throughout the docking-bay.

"Queil, this is Layroshk." He said, as his voice came through the shuttles comm-system.

"This is Queil" He responded, "Go on."

"Why have you not taken off?"

"I am in the process of doing so."

"Queil, there are three attack cruisers on the docking-bay, which will escort you to the Lork. They are three of the best fighter pilots among my crew, they will defend you with their lives if necessary. Now go quickly, I need you to be safely onboard the Lork if my plan is to be successful." Said Layroshk, as he watched the view screen, it showed both the docking-bay and the Draqkorlamaque mother-ship.

"Have a safe journey Layroshk." Queil said, as the shuttle and the three escorts began to move toward the docking-bay doors.

"As I hope you will as well." Answered Layroshk.

One of the escort attack cruisers was fired upon immediately after exiting the docking-bay doors, it exploded after taking three direct hits on the starboard side. The shuttle and the remaining two escorts were desperately dodging and weaving ships and energy blasts from both enemy and allied forces. Unfortunately, the only thing the dodging and weaving did was call attention to the shuttle. A Draqkorlamaque fighter quickly targets the shuttle from behind and fires several energy blasts, missing every time. One of the escorts then targets the enemy vessel and fires, hitting it on the engines, but it didn't explode right away, it managed to shoot and hit the shuttle on its stern section. Moment after, the same attack cruiser sacrifices itself to save the shuttle from yet another enemy vessel, which also had a target lock on it. Finally, both the attack cruiser and shuttle manage to make it onboard the Lork, but not without getting a

little bruised up, Queil is suddenly greeted and quickly taken to the bridge.

"Attention all vessels!" Shouted Queil, "Open fire on the larger Draqkorlamaque mother-ship, and no matter what the outcome, maintain course for Earth!" Everything was happening so quickly, that he didn't notice that the bridge of the Lork is identical to the Quern.

"How good of you to finally make it onboard the Lork." Said Layroshk, whose face was now on the view screen, "By now I am sure that you are aware of my intentions."

"Yes." Queil answered, as he sat on the captains chair, "And I still say it is suicide. How certain are you that, by colliding with the ship, it will be destroyed."

"I am not certain at all, but I do know that we may not get past them if

I do not try." They both then became quiet as did their entire bridge crew, "Just

remember what our mission is."

The screen then blanks out momentarily before it shows the mayhem happening outside. Queil watched helplessly, as the Quern headed straight for the newly built Draqkorlamaque mother-ship. He was horrified as he watched the ships he had ordered to assist the Quern, were being destroyed by the larger mother-ship. Within two minutes, over four hundred vessels were destroyed by the Draqkorlamaque armada. The bridge of the Lork was filling with smoke from all the firepower it was taking. A bright flash of light suddenly appears, it was the Quern colliding with the Draqkorlamaque mother-ship.

"All ships, evacuate the area immediately and head for Earth now!" Queil shouted to every ship through the comm-system.

Queil knew that the destruction of the two mother-ships would cause a shock wave, which would destroy over half of his fleet. The shock wave swelled then spread outward in all directions, he knew that his fleet would be overtaken unless he can think of a plan.

"All ships halt." He ordered, noticing that the shock wave began to dissipate, but still destroy many ships, "Helm, change course and position the Lork between the fleet and the shock wave. Place her vertically so that we take the full force of it."

"But doing that would severely damage our systems."

Said the helmsman.

"I am well aware of that, but I would rather suffer damage and delay our

arrival to Earth, than to lose over half the fleet." He said before giving one more order, "This is Commander Queil to all ships, get as close as you can to each other on the bow section of the Lork."

The ships began to get as close as possible, as the Lork positioned itself vertically. "All hands! Brace for impact!" Shouted Queil through the comm-system. A few seconds later the Lork shakes violently, as it took the impact.

It took a few seconds before the back-up systems were activated and the Quern was once again lit up, "Helmsman report." He said, but received no answer.

"The helmsman is dead, sir." Said a bridge officer who went to check why the helmsman did not respond.

"Then you take over." ordered Queil.

"But sir, I am not qualified for this type of duty." Said the bridge officer, as the body of the former helmsman was being carried away.

"As you can obviously see, we will not be going anywhere for quite awhile. All I ask is that you take that seat and give me a casualty report, I never mentioned anything about you navigating this ship. Am I making myself clear now." He said, leaning forward on the edge of his seat and pointed to the helm chair.

"Yes sir." The bridge officer replied, sitting down very quickly.

CHAPTER – 19

Suddenly a burst of smoke and fire exploded from one of the computer
console station on the starboard side of the bridge, which caused the crewman of that workstation to also catch fire. Several of the bridge crewmembers rushed toward the fallen crewman and assisted in extinguishing the fire and escorting him to the infirmary.

"Report crewman." Queil said to the newly appointed helmsman.

"There are casualty reports coming in throughout the ship, from every workstation and section. Life support systems are minimal on the lower aft section, but stable. The infirmary is reporting a large amount of casualties and are requesting permission to use the corridor, leading to the infirmary, as a triage facility. They are also requesting that anybody with medical training, report themselves to the infirmary for assistance." Reported the crewman.

"Very well, relay the medical assistance request to every pilot and crewmember. Order all of the damaged fighters to land on docking-bay one, also get the view screen repaired as soon as possible."

"Aye, sir."

"What about the status of the Draqkorlamaque fleet?" Queil asked.

"Long range scanners are detecting that the explosion has destroyed over half their fleet, and are not pursuing us."

"When will the engines be back online?"

"The engines were severely damaged, but they should

be operational

within several hours."

"Do you have any medical training?" Queil asked his temporary helmsman.

"Yes I do, sir."

"As do I and most of my people, but we are not familiar with Chabalarion physiology." He said, feeling a bit saddened about not being able to assist the chabalarion people in there time of need, "Go. I will take over your station till an experienced helmsman reports for duty."

"Thank you sir." He said while getting up from the seat.

CHAPTER – 20

Oubrago, Sandra, Maggie, Charles and, Lucille are on board the stolen shuttle, which has just passed Earth's atmosphere and are on their way to the Avoloxzia. "Does everyone remember the plan?" Oubrago asked as she made adjustments on the navigational console, causing the shuttle to reduce its speed.

"Yeah." Answered Charles, "We pretend that we're your prisoners."

"But what if they separate us, or even worse, kill us on sight?" Sandra asked as she sat on the empty seat between Maggie and Charles.

"Do not worry, I will not let them." Assured Oubrago, hoping that it would be enough to calm Sandra, as well as the rest of her passengers, who she could clearly tell were a little worried.

The Avoloxzia was less than fifty-five thousand kilometers from them and again Oubrago makes an adjustment on the navigational console, which causes the shuttle to change course. The mother-ship then sends an automated signal to the shuttles computer console that automatically increases their speed. Maggie hasn't said a word since she boarded the shuttle, all throughout the flight she's been almost lost in thought, not about the plan but about the first time she and her classmates took a trip to the Avoloxzia inside a similar shuttle.

"I think you should slow this thing down." Said Charles, referring to the shuttle.

"She can't." Maggie said, smiling with enthusiasm, "Just relax, I've done this before."

"Really? When?"

"During a high school trip. I'm surprised you didn't hear about it, the media televised it."

"Oh, yeah… I remember it now, every school throughout the world went." He said, while leaning forward to look at her, "So that would mean that you know the mother-ship just as well as Oubrago does? Am I right?"

"I'm sorry, but I don't." She answered while also leaning forward, "The Draqkor's only showed us what they wanted. However, what I do remember is the layout of the docking-bay and some of the corridors."

"That's good enough for me." Charles said as he leaned back and stared at the mother-ship.

"Please remain calm as we go through the Avoloxzia." Said Oubrago. If anyone were to glance over toward Maggie they would see a look of enjoyment as the shuttle traveled through the tunnel, which formed on the hull of the mother-ship. Charles, Lucille and, Sandra all covered their eyes in fear, but not Maggie. She felt nostalgic at the current situation because she also covered her eyes and felt fear when she first came to the mother-ship.

As the shuttle made its many left and right turns, as well as its ups and downs, Maggie let out a little chuckle that made Oubrago look back and smile at her. A few seconds later the shuttle stopped, and the scared passengers opened their eyes only to see Oubrago already standing and switching on her holographic device. She then opens the shuttle doors and her prisoners begin to walk down the steps, where two Enforcers are waiting for them. One of the Enforcers pushes Lucille very hard to the side, causing her to stumble to the floor. Charles suddenly shoves the other Enforcer to try and get to his wife, but the same Enforcer he shoved also pushes him to the floor.

"What is going on here!?!" Shouted Oubrago as she grabbed one of the Enforcers to prevent him from beating Charles.

"This prisoner became aggressive, he must be disciplined." Said the Enforcer.

"This prisoner, as well as these others, are mine. If they need to be disciplined then I, and I alone, shall be the one to do it."

Charles got up from the floor and assisted his wife up, all four were then pushed and shoved to form a line by the other Enforcer. "Go, move it." The Enforcer said.

"Where are you taking them!?!" Oubrago demanded to know.

"I am taking them to Zard for interrogation."

"No." She said, "I will take them."

"Why are they so important to you?"

"They are my prisoners. If Zard wishes to be generous and grant anyone a reward for the capture of these prisoners, then I should be the one to receive it."

"Very well then." The Enforcer agreed.

Oubrago shoved Maggie very roughly, causing her to nearly fall to the floor. She felt bad for shoving her the way she did, but she could not let her feelings show, it had to look as realistic as possible. As they walked toward the exit door of the docking-bay, with the Enforcers looking on, Oubrago would randomly alternate on shoving her prisoners.

"I apologize for my recent behavior." Said Oubrago as soon as the docking-bay door closed.

"Don't worry about it, I think we all knew what you were trying to do." Sandra said.

"Now what?" Charles asked.

"Now we make our way to the F.T.L. engine room. However, I feel I must apologize for any further shoving I will have to do should we come across any Draqkorlamaque Enforcer." Oubrago said.

The U.S.S. Roddenberry and the U.S.S. Reagan, have reached Earth and are orbiting it at opposite sides. Like clockwork, both spacecraft carriers dispatch space fighters to Earth simultaneously. The fighters were intercepted by Draqkorlamaque fighters, that quickly engaged in aerial and space combat. Earth's fighter pilots were responsible for not only defending Earth, but they also had to assist in protecting the spacecraft carriers which were immediately overwhelmed by alien fighters.

CHAPTER – 20

"Capt. De La Rosa, can you read me?"

"Go on Capt. Linwood." Answered Captain De La Rosa, "Why can't I see you on the view screen?"

"My bridge looks like Hell, we have taken too much damage and we have lost life support systems on three portside decks."

"Do you need assistance?"

"Negative. I'm sure your ship is taking quite a pounding as well."

"Yes. But unlike yours, we have functioning life support systems on all decks." Surprisingly there was no witty response, just static, "Capt. Linwood, can you hear me?" Still no response, "Helm, get a lock on the U.S.S. Reagan."

"Sir, scanners are detecting a huge explosion on that side of the world." Said the helmsman.

"Can you confirm if it was the Reagan?"

"Yes Sir, it was. The fighter pilots that were in the vicinity are confirming that indeed it was."

"Inform all fighters that the Roddenberry is in command and will coordinate this battle, also notify the Earth's Armed Force's of our current situation."

Captain De La Rosa wondered if the U.S.S. Freedom or the U.S.S. Sedgwick were in a similar situation and if so, how were they handling it. Suddenly the Roddenberry violently shakes and the bridge erupts with explosions, "Helm, report."

"Damage reports are being reported from every deck, we're losing power and rapidly descending into Earth's atmosphere." Responded the helmsman.

"Where exactly are we descending to?"

"We will be descending somewhere over the Atlantic within thirty minutes."

"Will it be a controlled descend?" Asked the Captain.

"Yes, up until we impact with the ocean." The helmsman answered.

"Have eight fighters escort and protect us on the way down." Said the

Captain, "Order all hands to brace for impact when necessary."

"Aye Sir."

"Also notify the U.S.S. Freedom and Sedgwick of our situation."

Capt. Wilkins' plan to attack the Draqkorlamaque mother-ship consisted of having both the U.S.S. Freedom and the U.S.S. Sedgwick come from opposite, flat, sides which were referred to as top and bottom.

"Communications, please notify Captain Lindquist that we will be within firing range in two minutes, and to have her ship, as well as all fighters, concentrate their firepower on the top or bottom of the mother-ship." Said Capt. Wilkins.

"Sir, we have just received a message from the U.S.S. Roddenberry." Said the communications officer.

"And?"

"They are reporting that the U.S.S. Reagan has been

destroyed, and that there ship has lost power and are, in what they hope will be, a controlled descend toward Earth's Atlantic Ocean."

"I see." He whispered.

Captain Wilkins sat quietly on his Captains chair, thinking of the thousands of crewmen onboard the Reagan, who have lost their lives. He wondered if the plan he had devised were changed, could their deaths have been prevented. His thoughts however, were cut short.

"Captain," Said the helmsman, "We are within firing range, sir."

"All ships! Open fire!" Shouted Capt. Wilkins.

Suddenly, like a swarm of wasps, Draqkorlamaque attack cruisers emerge from the Avoloxzia and intercepts the fighters. The two spacecraft carriers are the only ones firing at the mother-ship, while the fighters were engaged in spatial dogfights.

"Jiggy-J, how are you holding up?" Jason asked, as he fired, destroying an enemy ship.

"I'm doin' fine, but I can't seem to shake this one from my back." Jesus replied.

"I see you off my port-bow," Said Jason, "I'm on my way."

Jason reduces his speed and maneuvers his fighter behind the enemy and blows it from existence, "You owe me one Jiggy."

"That's a negative."

"Why is that?"

"That one was owed to me from the time you came back from Earth and hesitated on firing at the Draqkorlamaque ship, which was surely going to fire at you."

"HE IS CORRECT." Said Chrisash.

"No one asked for your opinion Chrisash."

Jason and Jesus fired at every enemy vessel that got in their way, sometimes assisting other fighters in need. They turn their attention at the mother-ship, firing everything they had with every fly-by. But like the spacecraft carriers, they're not making a dent.

Oubrago shoved her prisoners every time an Enforcer passed by them, always apologizing afterwards. Her prisoners, however, found it difficult to keep the charade going, especially Charles, who let out a little chuckle as two Enforcers walked alongside of them. Oubrago noticed that the Enforcers became aware of his laughter and before they reacted in a harmful way, she punched Charles on his lower back causing him to fall forward on his chest, where she then placed one foot on the base of his neck pressing his head against the cold metallic floor.

"Do not move human!" Oubrago yelled.

The ship suddenly shook violently, everyone either lost their balance or stumbled to the floor. The Avoloxzia continued to shake and rumble, but no permanent damage was being reported. Oubrago assisted Charles up off the floor and very quickly led them into an empty room, which was equipped with over fifteen computer consoles.

CHAPTER – 20

"What is this room?" Asked Sandra.

"This is one of many viewing rooms located through-out the ship." Oubrago replied, "It is used not only to monitor internally, but externally as well."

"You mean we can see what made the ship shake the way it did?" Sandra asked.

"Yes."

"How do we turn these things on?" Asked Charles.

"Everyone stand near one of the consoles and do as I do."

Oubrago began to press a series of buttons and switches in a certain sequence, sometimes pausing before touching another button. Each button had a weird almost hieroglyphic marking, making it impossible for a human to understand. One after the other, the computer consoles in the room were activated, some showing interior views while others showed exterior views. There were certain screens that showed different parts of the ship, such as rooms and cor-ridors. The images on the screens would change every few seconds, sometimes showing interior and exterior images si-multaneously in a split screen form. All five of them watched, at times in horror, as some of the images were of human people being tortured and even executed.

"There he is!" Lucille shouted, pointing excitedly at her computer console screen.

"There's who?" asked Maggie.

"My son!" She answered.

Charles quickly went over toward her to see, but it was too late, the computer console was now viewing another area, "Can we rewind these things?" Asked Charles, frantically touching several buttons, as if searching for that right switch.

"Yes, we can." Said Oubrago, "But please do not touch another button, for you may inadvertently reveal our location." She reached over and pressed the correct button.

"Wait, look!" Shouted Sandra, "This ship is being attacked!"

"Yes, and it appears to be attacked by your Earth's military." Oubrago said.

"That's fine and dandy, but can you find our son?" Asked Charles.

"Yes, of course."

"If you find his son, can you do the same for my brother?" Maggie asked.

"I will certainly try."

A couple of silent minutes go by, as Oubrago searches for the two specified prisoners. The other four, Sandra, Maggie, Charles and Lucille, watched as Earth's fighters were easily being destroyed. All four were unknowingly praying in silence for the safety of not only the military personnel, but also for their loved ones.

Oubrago, of course, had another idea, "Jason, can you hear me?" She asked, mentally trying to establish a mind-link with him.

"Yeah Oubrago, I can hear you." He replied.

"Is your squadron participating in that space fight out

there?"

"Yes."

"I am going to program the avoloxzia to identify you as a Draqkor so you can land and disable it from the inside."

"How do you expect me to do that, when I don't even know where to begin?"

"Do not concern yourself about that yet." She said, "We will meet you in the docking-bay."

"What do you mean by 'We'?"

"Your mother and Maggie, as well as your neighbors from across the street, are also onboard with me."

"What!?! Why!?! How!?!"

"I do not have time to explain at this moment."

"Well, can you at least let them know that I'm trying my best not to get killed out here."

"I will."

"One more thing?"

"What is it?

"Can you program the Avoloxzia to identify Jesus as a Draqkor as well?"

"Yes, but why?"

"I have a feeling I might need a little more help."

"Very well, proceed toward the Avoloxzia and be careful."

"I found him!" Maggie shouted, "I found my brother!"

"I also see you have found the equivalent to a pause button." Said Oubrago, looking at the screen in which Maggie was pointing to.

"Where is he?" Asked Maggie, "And what are they doing to him?"

"He is being held in a room not too far from where Charle's and Lucille's son is in." Oubrago replied.

"O.K. But what are they doing to him?" Maggie insisted on knowing.

"They are preparing to torture him till he dies."

"What!?! No! They can't!" She cried out.

They watched, as Jacob was held against his will on what seemed to be a flat, steel surface with straps binding his legs together by the ankles. His arms were also bound together, over his head, by the wrists. An Enforcer to his right was holding a thinly long, needle-like, sharp rod.

"What is that Draqkorlamaque planning to do with that thing?" Lucille asked.

"He is going to pierce it through his side."

"Is that all?" Asked Sandra.

"Yes… But that rod contains a lethal bacteria, which acts much like your acid does. It will dissolve an individual's internal organs, until there is nothing inside, within the hour."

"We gotta go and stop them!" Said Maggie, as she began to walk out the room.

"No." Said Oubrago as she held Maggie by the arm and stopped her from leaving, "We still have time to save both him and the boy, but first we must go back to the docking-bay and meet with Jason."

"How do you know if he's there?" Sandra asked.

CHAPTER – 20

"I communicated with him, telepathically a few minutes ago and he is piloting one of the fighters attacking this ship. He is not onboard yet but he will be momentarily, and we should be their when he lands to assist him with the Enforcers that are already there."

"Won't this ship detect him or something, seeing as how it's an Earth ship that's landing?" Charles asked.

"I have programmed the ship to identify his fighter as a Draqkorlamaque vessel." Oubrago assured them, "However, if we do not hurry the Enforcers that are in the docking-bay will destroy his ship before it lands."

"Let's go and make sure this kid lands safely, so we can go rescue her
brother and my son." He said, leading the way out the door, followed by the rest of them.

CHAPTER – 21

"Helm!" Captain Linwood shouted, "Whatever you do, keep the nose of this ship up!"

The U.S.S. Reagan has no power to help with its descend, instead the helmsman must rely on Earth's gravity and wind shear to glide the ship on to the Atlantic Ocean and hopefully land it there in one piece. The Captain had no doubt that the ship would stay afloat, he knew that if it could withstand the vacuumed pressure of space then it can also withstand the oceans water pressure.

"All hands brace for impact!" He shouted, praying that the designers of this ship, who modeled their design from an aircraft carrier, would be heard.

The ship, upon impacting with the oceans water, created a splash that could be seen as far as one mile. The ship sank forty-four feet underwater before surfacing, "Helm, status report."

"All decks are reporting minimal damage Sir."

"Good."

"Sir." Said the helmsman, "The aircraft carrier U.S.S. New York, is approaching us on the starboard side to render with assistance."

"Very well then. Send a message to all of our fighters

that we are still in this fight, also request the U.S.S. New York to deploy aerial support until we are capable of defending for ourselves."

"Aye Sir." Replied the helmsman.

"Also, if long range communications is operational send a message to Captain Wilkins and notify him of our current situation."

"Jiggy I need you to follow me." Said Jason, dodging and weaving Draqkorlamaque fighters, "We're goin' to board the mother-ship."

"What!?! Are you crazy!?!"

"Trust me."

"You think they're just going to open there door and let us land in there docking--" Jiggy couldn't believe what was happening, an entrance was forming on the lower portside of the Avoloxzia.

"Are you ready Jiggy?"

"Yeah." He replied, "I think."

"Alright, follow me." Jason led the way but upon entering the mother-ship, their fighters were no longer being navigated by them, they appeared to be automatically controlled by the mother-ship. All throughout the years that had passed since his school visited the Avoloxzia, he has always wondered whether the shuttles were put into auto-pilot or navigated. He finally had his answer, but with a new question: Their fighters aren't part of the Draqkorlamaque fleet, yet they were being auto-piloted through the various tunnels at great velocity. "How was this possible?" He thought.

"It is simple Jason." Said Oubrago through a mind-link, "I programmed the Avoloxzia to identify your fighters as a Draqkorlamaque ship, therefore safely guiding you through."

Oubrago, Sandra, Maggie, Charles and Lucille are suddenly cut off in the middle of the corridor in a gun fight with several Enforcer, preventing them from meeting with Jason and Jesus. Sandra shouts out a loud cry as she falls to the cold steel floor, holding her left arm in agony.

"Are you alright!?!" Shouted Charles, as he kept shooting at the Enforcers.

Maggie quickly rushes to take her out of harm's way, by helping her up from the floor and leaning her against the wall. She then tears off a piece of her shirt and uses it like a bandage to wrap Sandra's arm, which looked like she suffered a third degree burn.

"Oubrago we've landed on the docking-bay, it seems to be empty." Said Jason, still sitting in his cockpit, through a mind-link, "Where are you?"

"We are blocked off from the docking-bay several yards away, engaged in a fire fight with a squad of Enforcers."

"How do we get to you from here?"

"Scan my mind Jason and you will have a complete schematic of the Avoloxzia."

Jason stood on the wing of his ship glanced over at Jesus who was doing the same and closed his eyes, "I know exactly where you are and will be there in a few minutes."

"Good." Oubrago replied, "Now hurry, your mother has just been wounded on the arm but she will be fine."

"Quickly Jesus, let's go!" Shouted Jason, hopping off from his fighters wing.

"Go where?" Jesus asked as he too did the same.

"We're going to go to where my mother is and help her." Jason said, as he led the way out the docking-bay door.

"Wait! Your mother is here, onboard the mother-ship?"

"Just follow me."

Jason leads Jesus through a series of corridors making lefts and rights, as if he's done this before, all the while running. From a distance they hear fire blasts, they run even faster while reaching for their side armed pistol. They stopped just a few yards away, around the corner, from the Enforcers that were trying to kill Oubrago and the rest of them.

"Okay Jiggy," He said, as he gestured with his hand for him to cross to the opposite wall, "At the count of three, open fire."

"Got'cha." Whispered Jesus, mentally preparing himself for action.

"One…" He began to count, "Two…" They readied their pistols "Three…" Both give each other a quick glance before running and opening fire, and within moments the Draqkorlamaque Enforcers were killed.

"Oubrago, stop firing. We're coming towards you!" He shouted.

Jason bypassed Oubrago and everyone else to get to

his injured mother, who was leaning against a wall holding her arm in pain. He gently lifted her arm a little higher and with his other hand he firmly grabbed the injured area, within seconds the arm was completely healed.

"How did you do that?" Asked Sandra nervously, as she touched her arm and moved it around as if though nothing was ever wrong. She then removed the bandage and saw that her skin was like new.

"I'm not really sure." Jason said, "I just thought about your arm and the pain you must've been feeling at the moment, and it just happened."

"Do not fear your son Sandra, everything will be explained in due time."
Oubrago said, who noticed how uncomfortable and nervous she was getting, "However we cannot remain here, we must go now if we are to save the others."

"Others?" Jason asked, "What others?"

"My brother and their kid." Answered Maggie, pointing at Charles and Lucille.

Together they all make their way to the holding area where Charles and Lucille's son and Jacob, Maggie's younger brother were being held and about to be tortured. On the way there they didn't come across any hostile Enforcers, they were all too busy running to their designated duty positions. Once at the prison rooms door Oubrago points at Jesus and Maggie, signaling to stand at the other side of the door. Then she points at Charles, Lucille and Sandra, and signaled for them to stay behind herself and Jason who were at the opposite side of the door.

"There will be four Enforcers inside." Said Oubrago, "Jesus and Maggie will go in immediately after myself and Jason, then when all is cleared, Charles, Lucille and Sandra come in. But we must be swift before we cause any attention."

Oubrago is the first to go through the door and fires at the Enforcer farthest from the door followed by Jason, who fired at another Enforcer that was at the opposite side of the one that was killed first. Then came Jesus, who killed the remaining two Enforcers. When the dust settled, Sandra helps Maggie with Jacob, while Lucille and Charles went to their son. Oubrago is showing Jason and Jesus, from a monitor in the room, about fifteen other torture rooms filled with men, women, and children. Some alive, others dead.

"We have to help them." Jesus said.

"I agree." Said Jason.

"It will be difficult, but I too agree." Said Oubrago, looking back at the others, "However, what will we do with them?"

"That's simple, you take them back to the docking-bay, while Jesus and I go to free them."

"Wait!" Sandra shouted, "What's happening in the other torture rooms?"

"They are simultaneously being executed." Oubrago said. They watched in horror as the humans in all the torture rooms were being killed by a dozen or so Enforcers.

"That can only mean that they know we're here." Jesus said.

"It is possible." Responded Oubrago.

"What do you suggest we do?" Charles asked her.

"I suggest we head back to the docking-bay and get off this mother-ship." Said Maggie. As they made their way to the docking-bay, they ran pass many Enforcers, some of which ignored them while others tried to stop them, but failed in doing so.

"It appears we have intruders." Said Zard, as he enters the ships bridge and walks toward Beklota who was seated on his chair in the center.

"What!?! Why was I not informed?"

"It seems that the ships sensors were tampered by someone onboard."

"Then how did you know they were onboard?"

"While viewing one of the torture rooms, I witnessed them liberating two prisoners."

"How many were there?"

"There were six humans and one Drakkorlam."

"Where are they heading?" A very angry Beklota wanted to know.

"At last report, they were going toward the docking-bay."

"Zard, order fifty of my best Enforcers to meet me in the docking-bay. Inform them that they better arrive there before the intruders do." Said Beklota as he walked out the bridge to meet with his Enforcers.

CHAPTER – 22

Beklota and his Enforcers have managed to get to the docking-bay before the intruders, he stands by the door facing them and gives them a small subtle speech, "You all are my best Enforcers, the elite. But I say this to you all, if the intruders escape from this docking-bay then all of you will be executed." He told them.

"Commander Beklota." Said a voice through the docking-bay comm-system, "The intruders are moments away from your position."

"Enforcers! prepare yourselves for combat!" Beklota shouted as he hurried to the rear of the docking-bay.

Oubrago was leading them to the docking-bay and just when they get to the door, about to enter, she suddenly stopped. "I can sense them also Oubrago." Said Jason, who was in the back of the group.

"Sense what?" Jesus asked.

"There are many." She said telepathically.

"We can handle them." He responded in the same way.

"Hello? Isn't anybody going to answer me?" Asked Jesus.

"You do not understand. These Draqkor's are Beklota's elite Enforcers, they were genetically enhanced to be much more aggressive than any other."

"Enough with the silent treatment already!" Shouted Charles, causing everybody to look at him, "Now can anybody tell me why we stopped, when we're so close to getting out of here."

"Don't ask me how I sensed it, but Oubrago and I know we're about to walk into an ambush." Jason answered.

"Finally, an answer." Whispered Jesus in satisfaction relief.

"So what do we do?" A concerned Maggie asked.

"We go in fighting." Responded Oubrago, "But be careful, these enforcers are very aggressive and have the ability to move very fast."

"Also, Beklota himself is inside." Jason said.

"How do you know?" Jesus asked, "You know what, forget it. I don't wanna know."

"Jason, Jesus. Come up front with me." Said Oubrago, "The rest of you, cover our back."

They ran into the docking-bay and were nearly overwhelmed by the Draqkorlamaque Enforcers and, just as she said, they did move fast. Several Enforcers were killed immediately, but two of them managed to grab hold of Jacob by the arms and like tearing paper in half, they pulled his body apart just as easy.

"No!" Screamed Maggie in horror, as Jason reacts by killing the two Enforcers.

CHAPTER – 22

It's only then that everyone, including Jason himself, realized that he didn't kill the Enforcers with his gun but with his hand. A small, fist size, sphere of energy shot out from his clenched hand, hitting one of the Enforcers on the chest and the other on the head.

"How in the world did you do that?" Jesus wanted to know.

"Now is not the time for explanations!" Shouted Oubrago, "Focus your attention on the Enforcers!"

As Jason continues to fire at the Enforcers with both his handgun and his clenched fist, he notices a figure in the background. At first glance he thought the figure was another Enforcer but as they were being killed one by one, he got a better look at the individual and recognized him to be Beklota. He stood there, watching his best soldiers get killed by one alien and six humans. Every time Jason had a clear shot at him and fired, an Enforcer would take the hit, some did it intentionally but others were at the wrong place at the wrong time. By not being able to kill Beklota, Jason became frustrated and makes a run straight for him. But before he ran half a yard, Beklota himself made a run. However it wasn't toward Jason, it was toward Jesus. Before Jason could shout out to warn Jesus, it was too late. Beklota sneaked up behind him and plunges his fist into the back of his neck, ripping the spinal column out. The Draqkor leader ran out the docking-bay door, with the spinal column clenched in his hand, before the body hit the cold steel floor.

Maggie was the first to rush over to Jesus' lifeless

body followed by Sandra then Lucille, who kneeled on opposite sides of the body. Maggie gently lifted his head and slipped one leg underneath, to provide comfort, while sobbing uncontrollably at witnessing her brothers and one of her best friends cruel deaths. Oubrago and Jason were the next ones to be by his side, but they remained standing. Then came Charles, who stood guard between his son and Maggie, uncertain if all the Enforcers were killed.

"Is there anything you can do?" Jason asked Oubrago.

"No." She sadly responds, sensing the anger building within him, "There is nothing you could have done either."

"You're right." He answered her, "But there is something I can do now."

"And what's that?" Asked Maggie.

But Jason either didn't hear her or chose to ignore her, "Oubrago, make sure everyone here gets out of this ship and back Earth. I will catch up with you."

"Where do you think you're going?" His mother wanted to know.

"I'm going after Beklota." He said, as he began to walk toward the docking-bay door.

"I'm coming with you." Said Charles.

"No!" He said, "I'll do this alone." Charles noticed his fist glowing in a radiant sparkling light and heard a faint crackling sound, like wood burning on a fireplace, and quickly backed away.

"Jason." Oubrago mentally interrupted, "Do you

know where he went?"

"Yes, I can sense his thoughts." He responded, while walking out the door and killing every Draqkorlamaque that presented a threat or just simply walked by him, "It's as if he wants me to know his location."

As if taunting Jason, Beklota purposely drops pieces of his victims spinal column in every corner he turned till he arrived in front of the bridge door, where in english he writes on it, 'In here you will die.' before entering.

As soon as the Chabalar and Drakkorlam ships arrived, they immediately begin to attack the Avoloxzia and its fighters. They have divided into two forces with half going to assist Earth, while the other half remained in space. They quickly came to the aide of the U.S.S. Reagan, as well as many countries by providing air support and the deployment of soldiers from both worlds. The U.S.S. Freedom was receiving reports from Earth of how the Draqkorlamaque Enforcers were quickly being overwhelmed and defeated in some countries, which relieved Captain Wilkins, especially when he began to think about the situation that Captain Linwood was going through.

"This is Queil, Commander of this armada." He said as his voice was heard on every Earth, sea, air, and space fighter, "Is there anything we can assist you with?"

"Yes there is." Responded Captain Wilkins, "You could keep doing what you're doing."

"Very well."

***

Zard watched as Draqkorlamaque ships were being easily destroyed by this armada, "All ships, concentrate all firing power on the non-Earth ships." He ordered.

At that moment Beklota marched into the bridge, "I want no interference in what is about to happen from anyone, no matter what the outcome." He ordered, as he waited patiently on the other side of the bridge.

Jason enters the bridge and immediately runs toward Beklota, while at the same time shooting at him. He realized that Beklota was dodging and weaving every shot, surprised with how easy he made it look. When they physically make contact, the bridge crew watched and could not understand how Jason was able to move as fast as their leader. The Draqkor's observed how the human gave as much as he received but Beklota gains the advantage, when he scratched Jason across his back leaving four opened vertical wounds. Just as Beklota was about to give his final deathblow, by scratching him across the side of his neck, Jason quickly reacts, by unleashing a ferocious powerful blast of energy from his clenched fist, hitting Beklota at close range, in the head, causing it to explode.

As Beklota's body collapsed, Jason also fell to the floor in excruciating pain, helpless and becoming unconscious. Suddenly the ship shook more violently than any previous time during the attack, and Zard, who automatically assumes command, is in disbelief that a human has defeated a Draqkor. An Enforcer was about to finish killing Jason but was prevented by Zard, "Let the human be." He ordered, "He will die within hours, I want him to know that death is a painful journey. As for us, order the Draqkor's onboard to evacuate the Avoloxzia and head toward Earth."

The Avoloxzia is violently shaking from the impact of fire power that is originating from the unified fleet of Earth, Chabalar, and Drakkorlam ships, making it difficult for its crew to walk without stumbling. The impacts caused the electronics and walls to explode all around them.

Oubrago and the rest of the humans are onboard the same shuttle in which they arrived in, preparing to take off, when she suddenly senses what has happened to Jason. "I have to go." Oubrago said as she got up from the navigator chair.

"What!?! Where do you think you're going?" Charles demanded to know.

"I have to get to Jason." She responded while activating the holographic navigator.

"Has something happened to him?" Asked Sandra, concerned about her son.

"I am not certain." Oubrago answered, as she gave the automated navigator an order, "Navigator, lay in a course for Earth and seal the shuttle door when I leave till you get there. But be warned, the Avoloxzia is being fired upon, do not engage in combat, only evade."

"As you command." The navigator replied.

Oubrago hurried out the shuttle and ran for the docking-bay door, she heard the humming of the shuttle as it took off. She stumbles several times before getting to the bridge, where upon arriving she read what was written, in blood, on the door. She cautiously entered and was surprised to find the bridge empty, there wasn't a single Draqkor crewmember in sight except for the headless body of Beklota, which was a few feet away from an unconscious Jason. She knows what caused him to fall unconscious when she hoists his body over her shoulder, and notices the four finger scratches on his back. She goes as fast as she can to the docking-bay, and boards his fighter.

"I AM CHRISASH, WHO ARE YOU?" It asked.

"I am Oubrago."

"OUBRAGO. YOU SHOULD BE AWARE THAT YOU CANNOT NAVIGATE ME."

"Why not?"

"I HAVE BEEN PROGRAMMED TO RESPOND ONLY TO JASON'S D.N.A."

"Then if it is possible for machines to show emotions, you will be surprised by what is about to happen." She then touches the fighters controls and it responded.

"THIS IS NOT PART OF MY PROGRAMMING." It said.

"I will explain it to you on the way down to Earth." She said.

As Oubrago exited the Avoloxzia she saw familiar ships fly by her, firing at the mother-ship and all Draqkor-lamaque ships that came out of it. She worried if the others made it out safely, if they arrived back on Earth, but her biggest concern was whether or not Jason would live. Suddenly a bright light originating from behind was seen, indicating the destruction of the Draqkorlamaque mother-ship.

CHAPTER – 23

Jason is lying unconscious on the bed, nearly dead. He is surrounded by all his loved ones such as his mother Sandra, Maggie, Oubrago, and his Aunt Natasha, all of whom have been at his bedside for the last twenty-two hours or so, hoping that he will come out of what has been diagnosed, by his doctor, as a coma.

"Now, Mrs. Briggs, it appears that your son has been infected with some kind of bacteria which seems to be acting like acid, dissolving away his internal organs." Said the attending Doctor.

"So what you're saying is that there is no cure." His mother said, "That I will eventually lose my son."

"I'm afraid so." The Doctor said, "I've never encountered anything like this in all my medical years as a doctor, it's literally 'Alien' to me."

"Is there anything you can do for him, Oubrago?" Maggie whispered to her.

"No" She responded.

"From what your friend Oubrago has told me earlier today, Jason had approximately twenty-four hours when he came in. At the rate the bacteria has been eating away at his inside's, it would seem that your son very little time left."

"How long?" His Aunt asked.

"Perhaps two hours, maybe less." The Doctor said as he checked on his vital signs before leaving the room.

After a few minutes of silence Jason wakes up, "Mom…" He called in almost a whisper.

"I'm right here baby." She answered, as she hurried and sat on the edge of his bed. But as soon as she sat down, he became unconscious again. Sandra, realizing that she is about to lose her son without telling him how much she loves him or saying goodbye, bursts into tears.

Oubrago walks over toward Sandra and rubs her hand through Jason's hair, "Sandra, are you okay?"

"Yes, I'm fine. Its just that well…" She said, sounding a little choked up, "I can't tell him how I feel or how proud I am of him."

"Perhaps I can help you with that." Oubrago tells her.

"How?"

"I can transfer his essence into my mind, where he would exist for ninety-seven years."

"Are you serious?"

"Yes."

"Explain the ninety-seven years part?"

"My people have the ability to give birth to clones of ourselves every ninety-seven years."

"But how is that possible and how will you do that with Jason?"

"We accomplish this by genetically bonding, through

physical touch, with an individual who we may care about. of course the physical touch is non-sexual."

"You and Jason have bonded in this way already?"

"Yes… Ever since the day I first visited your home, when he came home feeling ill with the flu which I healed him from."

"That means that you're…" Sandra couldn't bring herself to finishing her sentence.

"Yes, I am what you call pregnant." Oubrago answered, "But he will be reborn as a fully grown adult, seventy-five years from now."

"Will he remember us?" Natasha asked.

"Yes. His memory will remain intact." She assured the both of them, "But I will only proceed with your permission Sandra."

"Yes, please. You have my permission."

Oubrago places two finger from each hand on Jason's temples, much like she did in the alley several years ago. Jason suddenly wakes up on what appears to be a sandy beach unfamiliar to him, unaware that he was now in Oubrago's mind.

"Is the Heaven?" Said Jason.

"No, this is not Heaven." Oubrago answered, as she appeared out of thin air, "This is another part of my home world, Drakkorlam."

He looks around and notices that she was right, this wasn't Earth. "How did I get here? The last thing I remember was fighting Beklota on the mother-ship."

"You are not actually on my home world. In reality

you are lying on a hospital bed, in New York Hospital, dying from a bacteria that dissolves all of your internal organs within twenty-four hours."

"Wow…" Said Jason, dropping to his knees on the sandy ground in disbelief, "Is there anything you or the doctors can do?"

"No. But do not worry."

"What do mean 'Do not worry'?" He said, upset that she would even say that, "I'm about to die!"

"Yes, but you will be reborn."

"What!?! How? When?"

"Throughout the ten years since we met, you and I have shared a very strong genetic bond. My people only share that bond with one we care about, which causes the females to become fertile and give birth to fully grown twin clones of each other every seventy-five years. We then transfer our essence into the lifeless body."

"Let me get this straight." Said a confused Jason, as he got up from the ground, "What you're saying is that you're pregnant and will one day give birth to me."

"Yes." She answered.

"With a clone?"

"Yes, with a clone of you."

"And when will I be reborn again?"

"In ninety-seven years."

"That means that everybody I now know, will either be dead or very old."

"That is correct."

"So for the next ninety-seven years I have to stay here, on this beach?"

"No. Although you exist in my mind, all your five senses will feel as real to you as they have before. Any memory I have of my home world will be yours to explore freely, the seventy-five years I have mentioned will feel like six months to you."

"Does my mother know?"

"Yes, I have explained to her everything I have told you." She said, "In fact she is waiting to talk to you."

"You could bring her?"

"Yes." She answered as she slowly vanished.

As Oubrago vanishes his mother appears, crying. Jason, who has always had a soft heart when it came to seeing his mother cry, hugs her tightly. He knows how hard this must be for her, having lost John her beloved husband, his father, and now her son in the same hospital.

"A parent should never out live there children." She said, trying to hold back her tears for a few moments.

"I know mom, but I'm not dead." He tells her, as he held he face and gently wipes her tears away with his thumbs, "Are you forgetting that I'll be back."

"I know, but I will most likely be dead." She said.

"Oh mom, I love you."

"I know Jason, I want you to know that I will always love you." She said, taking a couple of steps back and vanishing just like Oubrago did.

CHAPTER – 23

Jason is now alone, wiping the tears which he held back from showing his mother. He looks up at the beautiful clear red like sky and notices something flying toward him. It was a bird, a very large bird. "The bird is a Chrisah." Said a familiar voice in the wind, "This one in particular is named Sulyse, the largest bird ever to exist in Drakkorlam." It was Oubrago's voice he was hearing.

When the bird lands he circles around it very cautiously, admiring not only it's size and beauty, but also it's rusty colored feathers. As he approached the head of the bird, he noticed the protruding fangs in the side of it's beak. He then stood on the side of the bird, slowly climbing on its back. Flying up into the sky, he shouts, "I remember the bird and thank you Oubrago…"

The End?

"Imagination Is Everything. It Is The Preview Of Life's Coming Attractions."
—Albert Einstein

Luis M. Cruz is physically disabled, diagnosed with Arthrogryposis at birth, which is Latin for curvature of the joints and muscles. But that doesn't stop him from following his dreams, or having fun. Luis is not only the Author of *The Day They Made Contact*, he is also the publisher of CRUZIN COMICS and Creator/Writer of *Jennifer the She-Wolf*, *Blood-Kill*, *Fuel of Life*: An Illustrated Short Story, *A.L.F.A.*, and *The Workout* - Erotica From A Handicaps P.O.V.: An Illustrated Short Story. All of which are available on Amazon and, Indy-Planet. While Luis loves to read and write comic books his passion, however, is reading and writing Science Fiction, Fantasy and a little Horror.

"The Publishing Industry, Like Everything Else In Life, Is All About Taking A Chance. One Either Fails Or Succeeds, But In Between Is Opportunity, Which Allows For One To Keep Trying."
—Luis M. Cruz

More from Luis M. Cruz

www.ingramcontent.com/pod-product-compliance
Lightning Source LLC
Chambersburg PA
CBHW071406100726
47908CB00004B/1074